Dear Julia

Amy Bronwen Zemser

Dear Julia

Greenwillow Books
An Imprint of HarperCollins*Publishers*

 Printed in the United States of America.
For information address HarperCollins Children's Books,
a division of HarperCollins Publishers, 1350 Avenue of the Americas,
New York, NY 10019.
www.harperteen.com

The author owes a debt of gratitude to the late Julia Child, pioneering spirit and servantless cook, who inspired a nation—and this novel—with her seminal cookbooks: *Mastering the Art of French Cooking,* 2 vols., by Julia Child, Louisette Bertholle, and Simone Beck; *From Julia Child's Kitchen, The Way to Cook,* and *The French Chef Cookbook,* all by Julia Child; and *Julia and Jacques Cooking at Home,* by Julia Child and Jacques Pepin.

The text of this book is set in 12-point Granjon.
Book design by Sylvie Le Floc'h

Library of Congress Cataloging-in-Publication Data

Zemser, Amy Bronwen.
Dear Julia / by Amy Bronwen Zemser.
p. cm.
"Greenwillow Books."
Summary: Shy sixteen-year-old Elaine has long dreamed of being the next Julia Child, to the dismay of her feminist mother, but when her first friend, the outrageous Lucida Sans, convinces Elaine to enter a cooking contest, anything could happen.
ISBN 978-0-06-029458-8 (trade bdg.)—ISBN 978-0-06-029459-5 (lib. bdg.)
[1. Cookery—Fiction. 2. Self-confidence—Fiction. 3. Best friends—Fiction.
4. Friendship—Fiction. 5. Mothers and daughters—Fiction.
6. Contests—Fiction. 7. Feminism—Fiction.
8. Family life—New York (State)—Fiction. 9. New Paltz (N.Y.)—Fiction.] I. Title.
PZ7.Z424Dec 2008 [Fic]—dc22 2008003824

First Edition 10 9 8 7 6 5 4 3 2 1

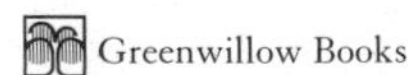
Greenwillow Books

For Lynnie

Part One

1

When Elaine Hamilton was six years old, she told her mother she wanted to be a cook when she grew up. At the time, her mother was trying to pass legislation toward equal pay for women. Elaine never forgot her mother's words.

"Oh, Elaine," she had said, hurriedly stuffing papers into her briefcase. "Can't you aspire to something higher? Twenty years since liberation and you want to stay home and slave over a burner?"

Elaine went into her bedroom, took out a sheet of paper and a pencil, and wrote a letter to her favorite person in the entire world: Julia Child.

dear Julia,

when I grow up I want to be a cook like you. Yesterday I made a sauce hollondaze from your ~~fee fessup~~ cookbook but I couldn't find a wisp of steam like you said and I think the yolks got to hot. The sauce sepuraded and I was going to throw it out but Dad said Elaine this is delishus. He pored it on his brockli.

love always,

Elaine Hamilton

Julia Child probably would have responded to this letter if Elaine had put it in the mail. But this was the funny thing: Elaine was much too shy a child to actually send this letter, or any of the letters she had written over the years to her favorite person in the entire world. Instead she locked them inside an old wooden chest with brass handles at the foot of her bed, and she never spoke again of her dream to become a cook. But from the time she was six years old, she always got up before her parents and three younger brothers to fix breakfasts and school lunches, and by the end of the second grade, she was preparing French-inspired dinners. On her eighth birthday, Elaine's father bought her a box set that contained the titles *Mastering the Art of French Cooking, Volume One* and *Volume Two*, and by the time Elaine was in the third grade, she was preparing meals with wonderful names like Poulet Poché au Vin Blanc and Caneton Rôti à l'Alsacienne for the entire family.

Elaine's brothers hardly noticed the meals, as they were often fighting about candy bars or getting the bus on time or who hit who first, and her mother was too busy consensus-building with colleagues to notice. But Elaine's father, who stayed at home, raised the children, and practiced vinyasa yoga in the basement, always took his meals with great relish.

"Delicious, Elaine," he said, when Elaine was in first grade and made an onion tart with anchovies and black olives. "Just delicious."

"So tasty," Mr. Hamilton said, when she made a Soufflé Vendôme, a *soufflé* with poached eggs, in second.

"Marvelous," her father said, closing his eyes and spooning up a mouthful of Crème Pâtissière. "Simply marvelous."

As Elaine grew older she made a study of Julia Child's

cookbooks, and her repertoire expanded to include dishes that required many steps, such as Filet de Boeuf Rôti, Sauce Périgueux, or Thon en Chartreuse *(tranches de poisson en chartreuse)*. And as the years went by, Elaine continued to write letters to Julia Child, although as she grew older her questions became more nuanced. In the sixth grade, Elaine wrote:

. . . regarding the larding and marinating of the beef, the *lardoir* I have chosen is eleven inches long and has a hinged point that I understand serves as a handle. While you have suggested buying the needle with the longest blade, I tend to find the shorter blade with the removable handle far more preferable. Will there be a problem with the snugness of fit in a handle a few inches shorter than your ideal? Additionally, while I of course larded my roast in the direction of the grain, I did not necessarily hold fast with a counterclockwise rotating pattern and was wondering if you . . .

Of course Julia Child never responded to any of these letters because Elaine sealed and stamped them, and put them on top of the now hundreds of other letters she had sealed and stamped and locked away in her wooden chest with the brass handles. So it went this way for years and more years, with Elaine cooking more and more amazing dishes for what grew to be five brothers (when Elaine was ten, her mother had twins), and for her mother, who barely paid attention because she was concerned about her constituency, and for her father, who would close his eyes, fork up another bite of *pâté de campagne*, and say, "Delicious, Elaine. Just delicious."

By the time Elaine turned sixteen, she had memorized nearly every recipe and mastered every technique that Julia Child knew, and she had secretly decided to apply to Smith College in Northampton, Massachusetts, which Julia Child had attended in the 1930s. After college, Elaine would fly to Paris to earn a cooking degree at the Cordon Bleu (which Julia Child had also attended), and after that she had plans, like Mrs. Child herself, to become a great cook and teacher. She did not tell anyone of these dreams, of course, particularly her mother, who expected Elaine to go to Dartmouth (which she herself had attended in the 1970s).

Elaine was a shy child who grew up to be an even shyer teenager, with large glasses and a ponytail that caused wispy fringes of hair to gather around her face. She wore a retainer to school. Her blouses were too loose, her slacks too tight, and her jeans cut too high at the waist. She had a tendency to use big words and complicated syntax, particularly when she was nervous. Although she was a naturally gifted student and her grades were excellent, she had no friends, as she spent all of her time clarifying beef broth, kneading dough, or teaching her twin brothers how to make a proper *ragout*. She was a wonderful teacher, patient and kind, if perhaps a little stiff. But she was only sixteen.

Meanwhile, growing up in the very same town at the very same time, and attending the very same high school as Elaine Hamilton, there lived a girl named Isadora Wilhelminetta Fischburger, a name that was so terrible she changed it to Lucida Sans, which is the name of a font on the computer (a font that Isadora, or Lucida, as we shall now call her, thought was the most beautiful name in the entire world). Lucida was the outgoing, talkative, and dreamy only child of two mothers. Elaine knew vaguely of Lucida and Lucida knew vaguely of Elaine, but they didn't travel in the same circles and never found occasion to talk to each other. While Elaine was keeping to herself, Lucida was preoccupied with getting attention—and lots of it—because her life's ambition was to become extremely rich and famous, with an emphasis on famous. She had no idea how she wanted to become famous —and the truth was, if you asked her she would tell you that it didn't matter how, just that she must become famous. Period. So Lucida spent all of her time involving herself in activities that would lend themselves well to fame. For example, in the third grade she tried her hand at baton in the hopes that she would someday lead the Macy's Thanksgiving Day Parade, and the following year she took up ballet. In fifth grade she was given singing lessons until the teacher suggested modern dance, and then it was tap and jazz until the sixth grade, and so on and so forth. In junior high she auditioned for roles in school productions, but she wasn't a very good actor, so she rarely got good parts. She was also unathletic and uncoordinated, which made involvement in sports difficult. The truth was, just about the only thing that Isadora Wilhelminetta Fischburger—aka Lucida Sans—was good at was trying to be good at things, and as you might imagine, nobody really gets famous for being good at that.

Like Elaine, Lucida was very smart, but she had few friends, namely because she loved wearing vintage clothing or wigs or period costumes, and she didn't care what anyone thought of her. Anyone, that is, except Croton Harmon, whom she had a weakness for, on account of his extreme handsomeness. But we will get to that later. Like

Elaine, Lucida spent most of her time by herself, perfecting her craft, whatever particular craft she happened to be working on perfecting at that particular time.

Elaine and Lucida met on a warm day in late September, just a few weeks into their junior year in high school. It was a Sunday afternoon, the day of the New Paltz Festival on the Green, one of the biggest town fairs of the year. Mrs. Hamilton was one of the committee organizers and she, along with the mayor and several members of the town council, stood at an entrance festooned with flowers and balloons, greeting members of the community and asking people to vote yes on local proposition seventeen and a half. Beyond the entrance, lining the perimeter of the green, were about forty or so commercial exhibitors, arts and crafts vendors, clothing sellers, and food and ice-cream stands. There were kiddie rides and face-painting tents, lemonade stands—even a pie-eating contest. Someone was selling sandwiches out of a refurbished golf cart that went around and around the green. Elaine and her five brothers were supposed to stand at their mother's booth, introduce themselves to voters, and hand out pamphlets detailing their mother's challenges to the current administration.

Unfortunately, Elaine was standing at the table by herself. The twins had long since run off to fish for magnetic ducks, and the rest of her brothers wandered away in search of ice cream. Elaine, characteristically uncomfortable with greeting people, was instead gazing longingly at a nearby booth with vertical bands of blue, white, and red going all around the canopy. The banner in front of the tent read JUS LIÉ in bold letters, which was the name of the finest French restaurant in the Hudson Valley. Gerard Etienne, a certified chef and the owner of Jus Lié, was doing a cooking demonstration with his son, Marceau, who was Elaine's age and apprenticing in his father's restaurant. Both father and son wore chef's whites with the insignia JUS LIÉ embroidered into the shirt.

Elaine watched Marceau bathe *crêpes* in orange butter inside a chafing dish, carefully folding them and layering them with long utensils so they absorbed the heat and sugar.

Robyn, one of Elaine's twin brothers, wandered over.

"What are they making, Elaynee?" he asked.

"*Crêpes Suzette*. Shh."

Marceau held a bottle of cognac in one hand and Grand Marnier in the other. With great flair, he smiled for the crowds and poured streams of alcohol from both bottles onto his *crêpes*. At the skillet next to him, his father did the same.

"Very dangerous," Elaine told her brother. "Fire can leap up the stream of alcohol and shatter the bottle."

Gerard Etienne lit a match and the *crêpes* burst into flames. The audience applauded. Marceau spooned the blue liquid over the *crêpes* and served them on paper plates to members of the audience.

"Wow, Elaynee."

Elaine sighed. She wished her father were a master chef rather than a stay-at-home dad who practiced vinyasa yoga in the basement. She took her brother's hand.

"Flambéing requires skill," she said. "But someday I'll teach you the method." Robyn nodded and ran off to try a *crêpe*, and Elaine returned to the table with the pamphlets. Her mother appeared.

"Elaine," she said. "I don't see you greeting anyone."

"No one has stopped by," Elaine replied.

Elaine's mother was wearing a blue double-breasted pants suit and alligator heels. She looked distracted.

"Where are your brothers?"

Elaine shrugged. She looked past her mother at Jus Lié, trying to see if Marceau's father folded his *crêpes* in one layer or if perhaps he overlapped them on the side of the pan.

". . . as I said, Elaine, please try and look presentable. Tuck in your shirt. Where is your father? Oh, there's Bob Edward, I've got to speak to him about that family leave bill." She turned back and pushed a few wisps of hair away from Elaine's face. "Try and represent this family with pride, all right, Elaine? For me?"

Elaine nodded. Her mother walked away. Elaine was about to take a few steps closer to Jus Lié when she noticed in the middle of the green, not far away, a few high-school students from the drama department carrying a set of wooden steps to one side of a raised stage. They were wearing buckled shoes and breeches and caps with feathers sticking out, and they were carrying cardboard trees and shrubs. A very handsome boy in pink tights and billowy pants was lifting an enormous painting of a stone house with a square cut out to look like a balcony. Elaine watched the handsome boy for a moment—he was, in fact, very handsome, with black hair and creamy skin and a perfectly square jaw—until she realized that he was just one of the drama students from school, and since Elaine neither cared about nor was interested in acting, she turned back to the cooking demonstration. There was something peculiar about the handsome boy's eyes that stayed in Elaine's mind, however, and just as she was about to reach into her pocket for her spectacles to get a closer look, a girl in an Ethel Merman wig rushed over, blocking her view. The girl was wearing a striped green dress with bell-shaped sleeves and a ruffled neck.

"Is it sturdy?" she asked the handsome boy. She disappeared behind the painting of the stone house and reemerged at the top through the cutout balcony.

"Is that supposed to be Juliet?" someone near Elaine asked.

"Helluva Juliet," someone else snickered.

In addition to her bell-shaped sleeves and ruffled neck, Juliet (otherwise known as Isadora Wilhelminetta Fischburger, or Lucida Sans) wore sequined heels and a neon green feather boa. She ran up and down the stairs behind the cardboard, telling the other actors where to put the trees and shrubs, and arranging the paper flowers in the garden. The handsome boy in the pink tights got into an argument with Lucida and began waving his hands around, but they were too far away for Elaine to hear. At some point they looked ready to begin. Someone plugged in a microphone, and Lucida approached the stage.

"Ladies and gentlemen," she began, and adjusted her wig. Feedback from the microphone made a shrill whistling noise. Several people at the lemonade stand stopped talking and looked around. Lucida fiddled with the microphone and tossed the feather boa over her shoulder. She cleared her throat.

"Ladies and gentlemen," she repeated. "The drama department of New Paltz High School proudly presents a few scenes from William Shakespeare's *Romeo*"—and here she paused to point to the handsome actor in the pink tights, who bowed grandly for the audience—"*and Juliet*," she finished, pointing to herself and curtseying, then bowing, then curtseying again. She returned to the microphone and added, "A tragedy written by"—she paused and frowned at the crowd, which was dispersing rapidly—"William Shakespeare."

Somebody whistled. Two people clapped their hands. Lucida fiddled for a few moments with the microphone, which made a deafening sound. She shook it roughly, tapped the top of it, then shrugged her shoulders and tossed it into the grass in front of the stage. She went around behind the cardboard scenery and appeared at the top, situating herself behind the cutout painting of the balcony. A bit of her feather boa dangled out the window and floated in the breeze.

The handsome boy got down on one knee at the base of the cardboard balcony. He tilted his head in Lucida's direction. He didn't look lovestruck, the way Romeo is supposed to be in the balcony scene. He looked mad.

"Romeo, Romeo," Lucida began, tugging at her wig. She leaned out of the cardboard window to continue, but the panel made a funny groaning sound, buckled, and fell over, squashing Romeo so completely that only the feather in his cap stuck out from beneath the scenery. Two other actors rushed onto the stage, but in their haste they knocked over a tree and three shrubs. Someone fell off the stage and landed on the microphone in the grass, which made a reverberating sound so shrill and piercing that a man across the green, who was pouring gasoline through a funnel into his refurbished golf cart, jumped three feet into the air. Gas sloshed into the grass and met with a lit cigarette that someone was about to stamp out. A small fire broke out in the dry grass and met with a cable leading to a generator charging the Jump Sac.

What happened next is hard to describe. A fire started in the Jump Sac (thank goodness there were no children bouncing in it) and spread to a clothing tent next door, setting a rack of dresses and silk shirts ablaze before moving on to a booth filled with antique quilts. Flames devoured each vendor's booth, leaving screams and smoking canvas behind. At the striped booth belonging to Jus Lié, Gerard

Etienne was pouring cognac and orange liqueur into the skillet of *Crêpes Suzettes* when he noticed the approaching blaze, let out a very high scream, dropped the *Suzettes* and the liquor bottles, and knocked over the butane gas flame. There was an explosion and a huge puff of smoke. The whole thing took about ten seconds.

Amazingly, no one at the New Paltz Festival on the Green was seriously hurt. The fire department arrived, of course, along with police crews and the local news, and it wasn't long before people recovered and began to clean up the mess. Lucida Sans answered some questions for a reporter and then went over to the lemonade cart in search of a cold drink. The cart, which was turned over on its side, wasn't far from Elaine's table of pamphlets. Elaine stared as Lucida leaned over and helped herself to a large cup of ice. Lucida caught her staring. Elaine looked away.

"What's it to you?" Lucida said, looking annoyed. She took off her feather boa, now scorched and black, and threw it on the ground.

"I beg your pardon," Elaine said, looking away. She began collecting her mother's pamphlets.

"It wasn't my fault," said Lucida. She slurped her lemonade and looked at the people packing up their arts and crafts and picking burned bits of canvas from their hair.

"Oh, but it was," Elaine said, her eyes wide with admiration. "It was."

"If Croton had listened to me about the set"—Lucida shrugged—"this never would have happened. He's such an idiot."

"You leaned over too far," said Elaine.

"What do you know about it?" Lucida demanded.

"Nothing," said Elaine, looking at the grass. "It was just—well, you created such a spectacle, I suppose . . ." Elaine trailed off and looked at her mother in the distance. She was holding the twins' hands and talking to a fireman.

"You thought it was a spectacle?" Lucida asked, looking at Elaine with renewed interest.

"Yes," said Elaine, relieved that she did not have to hand out any more pamphlets. "Quite memorable."

Of course this was all Lucida needed to hear. She took another big slurp of her lemonade and placed it on top of the sideways cart. She came over to Elaine's table.

"What's your name?"

"Elaine Hamilton."

"I'm Lucida Sans."

"As in the computer font?"

Lucida did not respond to this. Instead she stared at

Elaine and narrowed her eyes. "You look familiar. Are we in the same grade?"

Elaine nodded. "I'm in your homeroom," she said.

"Hmm," said Lucida. "How come I never noticed you before?" She leaned over to rub a burn mark off her heel.

"I don't know," said Elaine. "I suspect we don't travel in the same circles."

"Oh, really? What circle do you travel in?"

Elaine shrugged, feeling embarrassed, suddenly. "None, I suppose," she murmured.

"Do we have any classes together?"

"I don't think so," said Elaine.

"Just a minute," Lucida said. "I'm good at these things. I'm practically clairvoyant. I know I've seen you around somewhere besides homeroom."

"I don't think so," Elaine said.

"You're on the girls' hockey team," said Lucida, squinting her eyes and placing one palm on her forehead.

"No."

"Chess club?"

"No."

"Yearbook staff."

Elaine shook her head.

"I'm usually so good at placing faces," she said. "And

I read people very well, too, by the way. I was thinking about becoming a fortune-teller after I graduate. Palm reading and stuff. What do you think of that?"

Elaine shrugged. "Sure," she said.

"Hmm," said Lucida. "Well, it will come to me later, I'm positive."

Elaine didn't say anything. She could feel her shyness begin to overtake her. She started picking up the pamphlets and shoving them into a plastic bag.

"So what were you doing here, anyway?" Lucida asked.

"I was instructed to assist my mother," said Elaine, nervously.

"Let's get something to drink at the Muddy Cup," said Lucida. "I don't have anything better to do right now. They're going to be cleaning up this mess for ages."

"Don't you have to help pick up the stage?" Elaine asked.

"Oh, that," said Lucida. She looked over at the lawn, where three of the Shakespearean players were picking up soggy pieces of cardboard and throwing them into piles. From across the green the handsome boy who had been playing Romeo looked over and noticed Lucida standing there. He gave her a terrible look.

Lucida grabbed Elaine's arm. "Let's get out of here," she said.

This was how the friendship began. Elaine went with Lucida to the Muddy Cup, where they ordered cappuccinos and sat down at a table by the window and talked for quite a while. Well, more truthfully, Lucida talked. She told Elaine about her extracurricular activities, about her acting and ceramic classes on Tuesdays, her painting lessons and violin practice. She told Elaine about her obsession with the baton until the mayor ended up with a concussion at the spring parade some years back (Elaine remembered that parade, as her mother had been one of the organizers). Lucida spoke about her interest in sculpture and poetry, and about her involvement in the school's drama department since her freshman year.

"You're very busy," Elaine said when Lucida paused for a moment to sip her drink.

"Yes," agreed Lucida. "I think it's important to begin honing one's gifts at an early age."

"So what are your gifts?" Elaine asked. It was an honest question, and Elaine meant it in the most innocent of ways, but Lucida's face darkened and she screwed up her eyes.

"What do you mean, what are my gifts?" she demanded. "I just told you."

"Oh," Elaine stammered. "I didn't mean anything by that. I just—just—it seems as though you are involved in so many things. It's difficult for me to understand which one is exactly, you know—the main gift."

"Well, what are *your* gifts?" Lucida asked, in something of a huff. She removed her wig, a startling gesture since her hair was all pinned back close to her scalp, making her look almost bald, and placed it on the coffee table between them. It rested between them menacingly, like a small animal about to pounce.

"Me?" Elaine said, feeling intimidated. "I don't know. Perhaps I don't have any."

This was a lie, of course, but Elaine wasn't one to brag. Besides, she did not believe she had a gift for cooking. She only knew that she loved to do it.

"Oh, come on," said Lucida. "Maybe you're not as gifted at as many things as I am. But surely there must be something that you like to do, or that you're good at."

Elaine didn't feel like telling Lucida that she made breakfast for her father and brothers every morning before school. She didn't mention that she knew the recipes for twenty-two different sauces by heart, including the recipe for Sauce à l'Estragon and Sauce Périgueux. She said nothing of the dinners she prepared every evening, of the aspics and mousses, the *gratins* and the *savarins*. She did not tell Lucida that she could debone a twenty-two-pound turkey in under a minute. Elaine didn't like to talk about cooking with anyone but her father or her brothers, and she certainly was not willing to share her lifelong dream of becoming a chef and teacher with a near stranger. Elaine was ashamed of her dream because, as her mother had pointed out so many years ago, her ambition was of a domestic nature and had little to do with furthering the cause of gender equality or deconstructing traditional family roles.

"No, I'm not good at anything," Elaine said finally.

"Well, that's ridiculous," said Lucida. "Everybody is good at something."

Elaine shook her head.

"What about a wish, then? Do you have a secret wish? A dream you could be something?"

Elaine shook her head again.

Lucida took another sip of her cappuccino. "I have a thousand wishes." She sighed. "You can have one of mine." She brightened. "Hey, do you want to come over for dinner tomorrow night?"

"Are you referring to your house?"

"Sure my house," Lucida said. "What do you think? You could come for supper and meet Moms."

Elaine thought it over for a second. "Sure," she said. "Why not."

Dear Julia,

In your book you rote after watching two soufflés rise, you will be Konfident enouff to set the timer and walk away. I made eighty-three in my life so far, but I always watch them rise. Becose I am skared they will fall. When will I be Konfident enouf to set the timer and just walk away?

Sincerely,

Elaine Hamilton

2

At four o'clock the following afternoon, just as Elaine was removing giblets from a raw bird, the telephone rang.

"Are you coming?" Lucida asked.

"Yes." Elaine balanced the phone on her shoulder and tilted her head so she could keep her hands free to work. "What time am I expected?"

"We usually eat at seven."

Elaine didn't answer right away. She didn't know how to tell Lucida that she wasn't sure she could get to her house by seven. She hadn't finished preparing the bird, and she still needed to make bread crumbs for the stuffing.

"Yoo-hoo, anyone home?"

"Yes, I'm here."

"So I'll see you then? Good." And before Elaine could think of anything to say, Lucida hung up. Elaine removed the rest of the chicken innards and put them on a small plate. Then, as she sliced a French loaf, the phone rang again.

"Better make that seven thirty," Lucida said. "In case my parents get home later."

"I don't know—" said Elaine, struggling to hold the phone. But Lucida was no longer on the line.

Elaine sautéed the chicken gizzard in hot butter and oil for two minutes, then added the heart and liver. She minced a shallot. She was just transferring the mixture to a large bowl when the phone rang a third time.

"On second thought," Lucida said. "Better make it seven. We don't want to be up too late on a school night. I have to be fresh for auditions tomorrow."

"Auditions?" Elaine asked, placing four pieces of bread into the blender and turning it on.

"Is someone vacuuming over there?"

Elaine shut off the blender and stirred the crumbs. "Sorry? Oh, yes, the—the vacuum."

Lucida hung up. Elaine added cream cheese and butter to the bread crumbs and mixed everything together. She measured tarragon, removed the leaves from a sprig of thyme, and rough-chopped some parsley. She was just adding salt and fresh ground pepper when the phone rang again.

"A thought crossed my mind," Lucida said. "Do you know where I live?"

"I don't."

"Well, it's one hundred Elting. Just past the park. It's probably a ten-minute walk from you." There was a pause. "Where do you live?"

"Juniper Street. By the elementary school."

There was silence on the other end of the line.

"Of course, it might be something of a longer walk," Lucida said. Elaine thought she heard Lucida's nails clicking against the phone. "You don't by chance happen to know how to drive, do you?"

"Yes, but—"

"Oh, good. So go straight down Sunset, take a left on Chestnut, a left on Front Street, cross Main, and then go along Plattekill for a few minutes. When you see a big tree, go right. When you see a university building, go right. When you see a fire hydrant, go left—"

"I'm not—I'm not an experienced driver, I—"

"That's okay. There won't be much traffic. Bye." Lucida hung up again.

By Lucida's fourth call, Elaine had already set aside the stuffing and was shelling fresh peas into a porcelain bowl.

"I feel I must tell you," Lucida began.

Elaine finished with the peas and filled a skillet with cold water from the sink.

"My family. My parents, really. They're kind of unusual."

Elaine did not know how to respond to this. She already regarded her own family as strange. Could other families be as unusual as her own?

"I mean, my parents are not the regular type of parents, if you know what I mean."

Elaine did not know what Lucida meant at all, but her primary concern at this point was getting dinner prepared by six ten, since she now understood there was a fifty-minute walk to Lucida's ahead of her. Her five brothers would be home at five thirty, her mother at five forty-five, and her father, well, her father was always home. She worried that he would ruin the meal without her there to save him from forgetting to baste or season or salt something.

"Are you still there?"

"Yes, I'm here." There was another long pause, during which Elaine peeled three white onions.

"Just keep an open mind," Lucida said finally.

"All right."

But of course Lucida had hung up already. Elaine put down the phone and peeled eighteen more onions. Then she went to the pantry to look for a piece of cheesecloth to make an herb bouquet. By five thirty, the onions were simmering and the green peas were at a rapid boil. By five thirty-five, she had filled the chicken with her giblet and bread-crumb stuffing, and sewed the vent with her trussing needle. At five forty, her father came up from the basement. He was drenched in sweat.

"Smells fantastic, Elaine," he said. "What's cooking?"

"Poulet Rôti à la Normande," Elaine said. Then, before her father could ask, she added, "Roast chicken with cream, herb, and giblet stuffing."

"Ah."

"Garnished with freshly shelled peas and white pearl onions," Elaine added.

"White pearl onions," her father repeated, wiping his forehead with a dish towel. "Do they come in other colors?"

"Dad," said Elaine, rather nervously.

"Yes, my love?"

"I have been invited to an engagement this evening that prohibits me from fulfilling my obligation to this meal. Of course I would understand completely if you do not allow me to go." Elaine turned down the heat beneath the peas and looked at her father.

"Well, I don't know, Elaine," said her father, smiling a little as he pulled out a chair at the kitchen table. He was wearing blue tights and a shirt without sleeves. His face was red from yoga poses. "What sort of engagement is this?"

"A friend at school invited me to dinner with her parents."

"I see. And does this friend have a name?"

"Lucida," Elaine said. "Her name is Lucida Sans."

"Lucida Sans. I don't know anyone by that name, and yet it sounds so familiar." He scratched the back of his neck and ran his fingers through his hair.

"I must leave at six ten so as not to be late."

"What time's the dinner?"

"Seven."

"Where does she live, Europe?"

"Elting Street. By the park."

"Well, that's all the way across town, Elaine. Why are you walking?"

"It is my preferred mode of transportation," Elaine replied.

"Nonsense. Take the car."

"It is my preferred mode of transportation," Elaine repeated.

"Well, how silly." Elaine's father got up and looked at the chicken, neatly stuffed and trussed, and ready to go into the oven. "It will take you more than fifty minutes to get to the park, Elaine. You'd better leave by six if you want to be there on time."

Elaine hesitated. The peas were nearly done, and the seasoning would be easy. She could drain them and instruct her father to heat them later. But the Poulet Rôti à la Normande was a little harder to explain.

"I'll handle dinner, Elaine. You go on upstairs and change out of that apron."

"Of course I would understand completely if you do not allow me to go," Elaine repeated awkwardly.

"Not only am I allowing you to go," said Elaine's father, turning the oven to 350 degrees, "I am ordering you to go."

"Don't let the liquid stock fully evaporate from the onions," said Elaine.

"Got it, kiddo."

Elaine stood by the kitchen counter, fingering a dish towel. Above the counter was an iron pot rack that doubled as a shelf for some of Elaine's cookbooks.

"The bird should take no more than an hour and a half or so," she said.

"Excellent."

Elaine handed her father *Mastering the Art of French Cooking, Volume I* and removed her apron.

"Page 243," she said.

"Fine."

"Do not worry if the cream curdles in the pan."

"I'll try not to."

"You must baste every three to four minutes."

"Naturally," said Elaine's father, taking the cookbook from Elaine and squinting at the title. He put the book on the countertop.

"The peas are nearly finished."

"Elaine. Go upstairs and change your clothes. Live a little. Make a friend."

Elaine took off her apron and folded it neatly over the back of the chair. As she climbed the stairs to her bedroom, her father called, "You sure you don't want a ride?"

"The onions would dry out," Elaine murmured. She had just gotten all the way up the stairs and was putting her hand on the doorknob to her bedroom, when she heard her father drop a saucepan and mutter something incomprehensible. She sighed.

3

Even at a brisk pace in the cool evening air, it took Elaine an hour and ten minutes to get to Lucida's house. Twice she made a wrong turn, but this was not her fault. There was more than one fire hydrant along the way and, considering that Lucida lived by the park, a great many trees. Not to mention fire hydrants.

"You're a little late," Lucida told her as she opened the front door to a plain white house with brown trim. "But that's good. Moms aren't here yet." She led Elaine into the small foyer and opened the closet.

"I'll take your coat."

"I'd rather—I'd prefer not."

"Moms keep the heat up high. You'll sweat."

"I don't mind."

"Don't say I didn't warn you."

Lucida led Elaine down a short hallway to her bedroom, which had a pink door. The orange wig Lucida had worn to the Festival on the Green was hanging on a hook on the outside of it. When Lucida opened the door, Elaine saw a full-length mirror covered with polka-dot scarves and hats and wigs and beaded necklaces. There was an orange dresser covered with lipsticks and eye shadows and neckties, a set of false teeth, and what looked to Elaine, even from a distance, like a fake mustache. Shelves spilled over with books and feather boas and old album covers, and every available inch of wall space was covered with posters of opera singers, actors, ice skaters, politicians, and writers. There was a framed picture of Albert Einstein on the shelf over her bed. Above her desk was a black-and-white photograph of a stern-looking woman in a high collar.

"Is that your great-grandmother?" Elaine asked, looking at the picture.

"What? Oh, no, that's Emily Dickinson," Lucida said, kneeling down on a candy-striped shag rug to pull eight telephone books out from under her bed. She arranged them in the middle of the room, stepped onto one in the middle, and buttoned her white blouse to the top of her neck. Elaine stood awkwardly by the door in her coat.

"Think of this as a miniature stage," said Lucida. "Oh, wait a minute." She jumped off the telephone books and rummaged around her closet for a moment until she came up with a wig with a bun on the back. She put it on, and her face took on an angry, stern appearance. She looked out over the top of Elaine's head at an imaginary audience. Her eyes grew wider, and glazed over, as she spoke the words.

"Because I could not stop for Death,
He kindly stopped for me;
The carriage held but just ourselves
And Immortality."

"That was very interesting," said Elaine politely, when Lucida had finished.

"Thank you," Lucida said, stepping from her perch and unbuttoning the collar of her blouse. "Did you feel convinced?"

"Convinced?"

Lucida kicked the phone books back under her bed and threw the wig in her closet. She ran her fingers through her short hair, puffing it out, and sat back against her pillows.

"Yes. That I was Emily. It takes a lot of concentration to find your character, you know."

"Character?" asked Elaine. She was still standing with her back against the door, in her coat, not quite sure what to do with herself.

"Emily Dickinson, what do you think? She was a poet. I might have to play her on the stage. I should be ready."

"Oh," Elaine said. She thought this over. "I'm not familiar enough with the life of the artist to offer much insight," she said.

"Tell me what you think anyway. Did I look like a recluse?"

"I—"

"Did I seem in any way tormented?"

"Well—"

"What about genius? Was my rendering too obvious? A bit overstated?"

Elaine faltered, looked all around the room, and shrugged her shoulders.

"You looked as though you were hypnotized," Elaine managed finally.

Lucida wrinkled her nose and bit her bottom lip.

"Oh, well," she said, getting off the bed and going over to her desk. "Emily Dickinson wasn't famous until after she died, anyway. I have to set my aims higher. Or earlier." She opened the top drawer of her desk and pulled out a makeup case.

"The name of this color is Sherbet Sunrise," she said, applying the lipstick as she stared into an oval mirror on her desk. "It's very striking. Would you like to try?" She held up a plastic dispenser with little pink hearts around the sides.

"No, thank you. I don't wear makeup."

"Why not? You can really bring yourself into focus. I've been wearing eye shadow since I was twelve."

Elaine did not know how to respond to this.

"Why are you standing in the corner?" Lucida asked, swiveling herself around and staring at Elaine. Her lips were frosty orange. Elaine thought of the glacéed apricots she had made for her brother's birthday two years earlier.

"What time do you eat dinner?"

"Why, are you hungry? We could go into the kitchen for a snack."

"No. I was just—just curious. May I ask what your mother is preparing this evening?"

"I don't know. Moms usually order in. They're both

working all the time so there's never time to cook. Are you allergic or something?"

"No, no," Elaine said, looking into the stripes on the rug. She wondered how the Poulet Rôti à la Normande was coming out at home, if her father had properly braised the onions, if he had remembered to baste the chicken, to add mint to the peas. "I just—I was wondering, is all."

Lucida took off the sock on her left foot. She was wearing a toe ring that had a tiny clock on it.

"It's almost seven thirty," she said, tilting her head and looking at Elaine. "Let's go wait for Moms in the living room. I'm hungry, too."

"If you don't mind my inquiry," Elaine said, following Lucida down the hallway to the front of the house, where there was a moss green sofa, a mahogany coffee table, and a lamp. "Why do you keep referring to your mother as Moms?"

Lucida kicked off her slippers and settled down on the sofa. She motioned for Elaine to sit down, too.

"Remember when I said my family was kind of unusual?" she asked. She ran her hand along the arm of the sofa and wiggled the toes on her left foot. The clock on her toe ticked loudly.

"Yes."

Lucida was about to continue when the front door opened

and a woman with dirty blond hair and green eyes pushed her way in. She was carrying a grocery bag in one hand and a briefcase in the other. She looked harried and tired.

"Isadora," the woman said. "Take these groceries and go back for the rest. I've got to change out of these shoes." The woman put the bag of groceries on the welcome mat and wriggled out of her coat.

Lucida groaned and lifted herself with great effort from the couch. Elaine, unsure of what to do, wedged herself more deeply into the corner of the sofa.

"Don't put away the bread," the woman called behind her as she went down the hallway. Lucida went to the kitchen as another woman came through the door. This woman was shorter than the one with green eyes, and a little rounder. She was also carrying a bag of groceries and a briefcase.

"Isadora, come back for the next one," she called to Lucida in the kitchen. The rounder woman picked up the green-eyed woman's coat and hung it in the closet. Then she hung up her own. At some point between the carrying of groceries and the hanging of coats, both women looked into the living room and noticed Elaine, balled up in the corner of the sofa, trying not to look noticeable.

"Hello," said the one with green eyes. She had

changed out of her black business suit and was wearing jeans and clogs. "I'm Sue Fischburger." She turned her head in the direction of the kitchen. "Isadora!" she called. "Please put away the other bag of groceries, too."

"*All right*, Moms," Lucida called back, sounding disgusted.

The rounder woman came into the living room. She was also wearing a business suit, only hers was blue and a little more rumpled. She put down her briefcase and went over to the sofa.

"I'm the other Fischburger," the woman said. "You can call me Jean." She held out her hand to Elaine.

"Oh," Elaine said, trying to get up but somehow getting squashed in between the pillows and the arm of the sofa. "Oh. I'm—I'm Elaine. Elaine Hamilton." She pushed the pillow aside, and it fell to the carpet.

"Sorry," she mumbled, reaching forward to get the pillow. The other Fischburger—Mrs. Fischburger Number Two—leaned over and picked it up. She smiled at Elaine. Her eyes were so dark they looked almost brown, but in fact they were blue.

"No worries," she said. "No worries at all."

Lucida's two mothers had decided they didn't feel like ordering in that night. Instead they had picked up groceries to make dinner.

"Oh, boy," Lucida said to Elaine as they were setting the table in the dining room. "We're in for a treat."

Elaine watched green-eyed Mrs. Fischburger Number One and blue/brown-eyed Mrs. Fischburger Number Two work together to make dinner for Lucida and Elaine, all the while asking questions and making conversation in their warm kitchen. Lucida put her feet up on the kitchen table while they were talking and Mrs. Fischburger Number One told her to put them down immediately. Elaine pushed herself into a wooden chair as far as she could, but the warmth of the kitchen and the ease with which the Fischburgers spoke to her made her feel increasingly comfortable.

"So, Elaine," said Mrs. Fischburger Number Two as she twisted open a plastic bag of Wonder Bread. "Tell us all about yourself."

Elaine thought for a long time. No one had ever asked her a question like that before. She took the question very seriously.

"Or at least tell us where you live," Mrs. Fischburger Number Two added, glancing over at Mrs. Fischburger

Number One. She was rooting around in the refrigerator for something. She came up with a wedge of cheese covered in green fuzz and put it on the counter.

"I—I—"

"She lives on Juniper Street," Lucida said, rolling her eyes at Elaine. "And guess what. She walked here."

"She what?" said Mrs. Fischburger Number One, taking out eight slices of bread and laying them across the counter in a row. "All the way from across town? Isn't Juniper Street by town hall?"

"It is my preferred mode of transportation," Elaine said helplessly as she watched Mrs. Fischburger Number Two remove a carton of milk and dump the contents—soft white pieces that hit the sink with a succession of clomps—into the sink. She went back to the refrigerator and removed two heads of lettuce (they were black), some broccoli (it drooped), and a shriveled apple.

"Well, she isn't walking back," Mrs. Fischburger Number One said, taking out a butter knife and spreading each slice with an enormous slab of margarine. Mrs. Fischburger Number Two put a jar of mustard on the counter; Mrs. Fischburger Number One opened it, smelled the contents, and spread the mustard on top of the margarine.

"Mom, if she wants to walk home alone, that's her choice," said Lucida.

"And if I don't allow her to walk home alone, that's *my* choice," said Mrs. Fischburger Number Two, tossing three rotten tomatoes into the sink.

"We'll give you a ride after supper, hon," Mrs. Fischburger Number One said. She smiled at Elaine, who smiled back, weakly, and watched her spread mayonnaise on top of the mustard and the margarine. Mrs. Fishburger Number Two finally found what she was looking for—a very large container of cream cheese—and handed it to Mrs. Fischburger Number One, who opened the container and looked inside. She took out a spoon, cut around a portion of the cream cheese, and threw it in the garbage. Then she divided what was left among four pieces of bread and filled the container with water.

"Where's the lettuce, Jean?" asked Mrs. Fishburger Number One.

"Oh, I don't care for lettuce," Elaine said quickly. The two women turned and looked at her. "I mean, you need not bother on my account. . . ."

Mrs. Fischburger Number Two grinned at Elaine.

"All righty then," she said. "Fire 'em up."

Lucida took out an enormous frying pan and filled it halfway with walnut oil.

Mrs. Fischburger Number One floated the sandwiches in the oil and poured a glass of white wine for herself and for Mrs. Fischburger Number Two. Mrs. Fischburger Number Two turned the flame up high.

"The higher the flame, the faster the food cooks," she said to Mrs. Fischburger Number One, as a burned smell filled the air.

"Yes, hon."

Supper at Lucida's house was an experience. They sat together in the dining room and ate their deep-fried, blackened grilled cream cheese sandwiches and talked softly with one another. Mrs. Fischburger Number One listened very carefully when Lucida talked about her day at school and the arguments she'd had with Croton, who was still furious about the fire.

"He said there were talent scouts at the festival." Lucida sighed. "That I blew his chance to be discovered."

"Phooey," said Mrs. Fischburger Number Two.

"Hooey," said Mrs. Fischburger Number One.

"He's a rotten fig," said Mrs. Fischburger Number One. "A flower gone to seed."

"He's handsome," Lucida said, taking a big bite of her sandwich.

"He's horrible," said Mrs. Fischburger Number One.

"He's terrible," said Mrs. Fischburger Number Two.

"So handsome," said Lucida.

"A histrionic," said Mrs. Fischburger Number One, who had minored in psychology in college. "A histrionic, narcissistic borderline splitter."

"As listed in the *Diagnostic and Statistical Manual of Mental Disorders*," added Mrs. Fischburger Number Two.

"I know," said Lucida. "He uses me, too. Because I can work a camera."

"Get over him," said Mrs. Fischburger Number Two.

"Forget him," said Mrs. Fischburger Number One.

"I can't," said Lucida. "He's my weakness."

"Elaine," Mrs. Fischburger Number Two said. "Tell Isadora to stop thinking about Croton Harmon. There are nicer fish in the sea."

"But none handsomer," Lucida replied, taking another enormous bite of her sandwich. She sighed. "You'll never find a better-looking fish."

Throughout the meal Lucida's mothers asked a lot of questions about her school day and this teacher or that teacher. They wanted to know if biology class was any better than last week and if the history teacher's skin condition had improved. They were interested in everything Lucida had to say, and everyone laughed a lot and seemed to enjoy one another's company. Everyone also, Elaine noticed, spoke in quiet tones. There was an air of calm at the table, unlike at Elaine's house, where her brother Lynn would have been hollering that he didn't like his onions, or her other brother Chris might have been yelling because someone punched him in the arm. Elaine had only one mother, of course, but the one that she did have rarely asked questions. Even at the dinner table, she was much too busy reading briefs or worrying about this bill or that passing in Congress.

"How many brothers did you say you had, Elaine?"

"I'm sorry?"

"Did you say you had a large family, hon?" Mrs. Fischburger Number One asked.

"I have five brothers," Elaine said. She took a sip of her water.

"Six children," said Mrs. Fischburger Number Two, shaking her head. "How does she keep up with it all."

"My father tends to the family," Elaine said, nibbling on a piece of scarred crust. "He stays home."

"And your mother?"

"She goes to Washington all the time. She's very busy."

Mrs. Fischburger Number One looked over at Mrs. Fischburger Number Two.

"What's your mother's name, hon?" asked Mrs. Fishburger Number One.

"Elizabeth Hamilton."

The mothers looked startled. "Elizabeth Hamilton, the congresswoman?"

"Yes."

"Well, how wonderful!" said Mrs. Fishburger Number Two. "I don't know why I didn't make that connection."

"You're a celebrity, Elaine!" said Lucida, lifting one of the Moms' glasses of wine and taking a swig. "Here's to being famous in New Paltz."

"Put that down," said Mrs. Fischburger Number Two. She turned to Elaine. "You must be proud to have such an influential person in your family."

"Yes," said Elaine, and looked down at her plate. Nobody said anything for a moment.

"You haven't touched your grilled cream cheese sandwich," said Mrs. Fischburger Number Two.

"Can I have it?" asked Lucida. She picked up the sandwich from Elaine's plate and took a bite.

"Isadora!"

"She doesn't want it anyway, Moms."

"I—I really should go," said Elaine. "I hate to impose. And both Isador— Lucida and I must attend high school in the morning."

"Yes," said Mrs. Fischburger Number Two, looking at Elaine as she sipped from her wine glass. "Yes. Well, we must be on our way, then. Why don't you girls go spend a little time together while we clean up? Then I'll drive Elaine home."

"Really, there's no need, Mrs. Fischburger—"

"Nonsense. I won't hear of it. Go talk in the other room. We'll be done in a jiff."

"Well, thank goodness for that," Lucida said as she walked back down the hallway to her bedroom with Elaine. "Usually Moms make me clean up. They must be in really good moods tonight."

"I didn't know you had two mothers," Elaine said.

"I tried to tell you on the phone," Lucida answered, "but it's kind of hard to work into a conversation." She pushed open the pink door and threw herself on the bed. "Hi, my real name is Isadora—and by the way, did I mention that I have two mothers?" She lay back on her pillows and stared up at the ceiling. "They're okay, though, I mean, as far as mothers go."

"Why did you change your name?"

"Are you crazy? How am I going to get famous with a name like Isadora Wilhelminetta Fischburger?"

"I didn't know that you wanted to be famous," Elaine said, sitting down on the edge of the bed.

Lucida sat up and stared at the picture of Albert Einstein above her bed. "All my life," she said, and for a moment Elaine couldn't tell if she were speaking to her or to the picture of Albert Einstein. "All my life, ever since I was small, all I've ever wanted was to be somebody. To be somebody famous."

Elaine considered this for a moment.

"Famous doing what?" she asked.

"Who cares? I don't know. At this point I have to capitalize on all my talents. I'll specialize later."

"Oh."

One of the Moms—Elaine couldn't tell if it was Mrs. Fischburger Number One or Mrs. Fischburger Number Two—called down the hallway, "We're leaving in five minutes, girls!"

"Listen," Lucida said, sitting up and swinging her feet over the side of the bed. "The auditions for the New Paltz Revue are Friday after school. Do you want to come and watch me? I get so nervous. I could really use your support."

"What is the New Paltz Revue?" Elaine asked.

Lucida stared at Elaine. "You know," she said. "The Broadway revue. They do scenes from different shows. Don't tell me you've never seen one."

Elaine shook her head.

"Well, you probably haven't missed much. Ms. Thomas is such a wimp. She makes us do the revue every year because nobody can ever agree on one show. It's boring."

Elaine didn't say anything.

"I'm trying out for a solo. Last year they put me in chorus." Lucida scratched her eyebrow. "Come to think of it, they put me in chorus the year before, too." She brightened. "But I have a good feeling this year. Will you come? Please? Pretty please?"

"What time?"

"They start at two thirty, right after last period. In the auditorium. Come on, Elaine. Please come."

Elaine did not mention that she had a great deal to do that Friday afternoon. Friday was the day she went shopping at Paltz Produce & Co., the largest specialty grocery store in town. They sold farm-fresh vegetables and artisanal cheese. The market was on the other side of town, by the fairgrounds, and she always took the bus.

"It could be difficult," Elaine admitted.

"Oh, come on, please. I'm going to be so nervous.

Croton will be there, and he'll probably yell something during my audition because I ruined his chance to be discovered. And I'll probably laugh like an idiot because he's handsome, and he's my weakness. You could help me. You could give me a signal!"

"A signal?"

"Girls!" One of the moms called from the kitchen. "Let's go!"

"Yes. A signal," Lucida said hurriedly. "Like you could be in the audience, and if you see Croton is about to throw spitballs or yell something embarrassing, you could signal me. Like a cough or a sneeze or something. You could hold up a sign."

"Oh, I couldn't do that."

"I could look over at you. It would help me stay focused."

"Girls!"

Lucida got down on her knees and kneeled in front of Elaine. "Please? Please? Pretty please with a glob of deep-fried, grilled cream cheese on top? Extra crispy?"

At this point Elaine Hamilton did something that she had not done in a long time. Months perhaps. Maybe even years. She looked down at Lucida, who was still on her knees at the foot of the bed. She looked down at Lucida, and she smiled.

"All right," Elaine said, still smiling. "All right."

Dear Julia,

Now that I am almost eight I need to know how to make a good ~~ommelet~~ omelette. Today I burned eleven eggs! I was about to try just two more when my mother said Elaine Hamilton that is kwite enogh, time for school.

Sincerely,

Elaine Hamilton

4

True to her promise, Elaine stayed after school on Friday to watch Lucida audition. She planned to slip in from the back and sit in a corner seat, hopefully unnoticed, but Lucida spotted her as soon as she pushed open the door. She jumped up and down in her seat, waving her arms around and calling Elaine's name.

If Elaine were not so shy, she might have laughed at Lucida's costume, which was made of aluminum, chains, and tinfoil, and included (but was not limited to) a broom-handle horse, a helmet with a hinged flap, and chain mail. The outfit made an astonishing noise as she jumped up and down in her seat and waved her arms around in an effort to signal Elaine. Pieces of tinfoil fell to the auditorium floor. She lifted the hinged flap of her helmet so she could see.

"Over here, Elaine! I saved you a place!"

Elaine's face burned as she clutched her books to her blouse and watched her feet, one after the other, step down the aisle. Several students giggled.

"Over here!"

Step after step, step after step, Elaine thought of the batter she would make that evening for Gâteau de Crêpes à la Florentine. She had forgotten to add fresh nutmeg to her shopping list that morning. Nutmeg was essential for a good *béchamel*.

Lucida was in the last seat in the second row. Elaine had to make her way past eight students who did not bother to get up. The back of her pants legs rubbed against eight sets of knees as she walked sideways, leaning into the row of seats in front of her.

"Of all the rudeness," Lucida said.

Elaine tripped over Lucida's broom-handle horse and fell awkwardly into her seat. She tried not to notice everyone staring at her.

"Who's your friend?"

A boy in the front row turned around and regarded Elaine. It was the same boy, the one in the pink tights and billowy pants from the Festival on the Green. Now, up close and personal, Elaine could see his strong chin, his bright teeth, and a physique so beautiful it made you want to cry and hold your hand over your heart.

"This is my new friend," Lucida said. "Her name is Elaine. Elaine Hamilton."

"Nice to meet you," said Croton Harmon, giving Elaine a sullen look before turning back around.

Elaine observed once again, in that single moment, that there was something peculiar about Croton's eyes. They were not exactly the same color. One was as blue as a lake in summer, but the other was dark, almost grainy. The darker eye had a dull look about it, a cloudy quality that reminded Elaine of the way a fish looks when it is no longer fresh.

Croton turned to Elaine again. "Are you auditioning, too?" he asked.

"No," said Lucida. "You don't have to worry about more competition, Croton. She's my friend and she's here for *me*, for moral support. Something you don't know anything about."

Croton looked around to make sure nobody could hear him speak to someone as peculiarly dressed as Lucida. He leaned over the back of his seat and whispered,

"I'm going to get you back for what happened at the Festival on the Green."

"What?" Lucida asked.

"Nothing," said Croton. He turned around and leaned back, trying to look casual as he rested his long arms on the back of the chairs on either side of him. A blond-haired boy on his right and a girl with freckles on his left gazed at his profile.

"Yes, you did say something," said Lucida. "Elaine, what did he say?"

"Why are you talking to her?" the blond-haired boy asked Croton.

"Because he used to be my boyfriend," Lucida shot back at the boy. "What do all of you think of that?" The freckled face girl on Croton's left turned around.

"Is that true?" she asked Croton, shocked.

Croton turned red. "No," he mumbled. "I would never go out with a freak like her."

"Not publicly," Lucida muttered to Elaine.

Elaine looked at the floor. She felt uncomfortable sitting so close to the rotten fig himself, to be near this terrible flower gone to seed. When Croton turned back to his friends, Lucida whispered, "Handsome, right? You can't even *speak*, he's so handsome!"

The music teacher, a tall woman in a blouse fastened at the neck with a brooch, hurried down the aisle and clapped her hands together softly.

"All right children," said Ms. Thomas. "I'll take my place at the piano"—she motioned to the instrument, which hardly needed pointing to, since it was right behind her and in front of the stage—"and you may come up and take your place after I call your name."

Ms. Thomas put her hand to her throat and touched her brooch. She looked around at the students.

"Please remember," she said, as if just recalling the thought, "while there are many available spaces in this year's chorus, we only have a place for one solo part, so please do not—do not be discouraged if you find you are only selected for a part in the chorus."

She paused and touched her brooch again. "We try to honor and recognize every student, of course," she continued hesitantly, looking around. "For it is my dream that we, every one of us, will be able to spread the joy of our spirits and the gift of our—of our voices here at—" She paused again, looking around at the students, who were talking and passing notes and shooting spitballs at each other. "At New Paltz High." She sighed, turned to the piano, sat down, and put on her spectacles.

"Marty, do you have the list?" she asked.

A wiry boy with sandy hair came forward and handed Ms. Thomas a sheet of paper with a list of names on it. He bent over and whispered something in the music teacher's ear, and she scanned the seats for a moment, her eyes stopping when she noticed Lucida. She looked startled. Marty went back to his seat.

"Before we begin," Ms. Thomas said, standing up and walking away from the bench to address the students again, "may I remind you . . ." she coughed a little and cleared her throat. "May I remind you that not *everyone* makes the New Paltz Broadway Revue." She paused and looked around the room, again resting her gaze the longest at Lucida. She seemed to be speaking directly to her.

"What I mean to say is," she said, pressing her thumb to her temple and running a finger over one eyebrow, "some of us have talent for acting, others for dancing, still others, hopefully those of you here, for singing.

"Of course, if you don't make it to the chorus this year," Ms. Thomas went on, looking slightly flustered. "Well. I knew a boy who couldn't sing a note but was the first at the finish line in track and field at every meet."

"Ms. Thomas," someone wailed. "We're like, *so bored*."

The music teacher returned to the piano bench. "All

right, students," she said, looking at the top of her list. "Let's begin with Joanne Johansen. Joanne, are you here?"

Joanne Johansen appeared from one of the rows and climbed the steps to the front of the stage. She was skinny, with frizzy hair and braces. She handed over some sheet music, and Ms. Thomas began to play the introduction to "Let Me Entertain You." Joanne's knobby knees shook as she danced.

"Wow," said Lucida.

Elaine nodded.

The auditions went on. A freshman boy sang "Climb Every Mountain," and a football player in uniform finished his rendition of "Somtimes I Feel Like a Motherless Child" with three somersaults and a triple back flip. Everyone cheered. Other students came and went. Finally, Ms. Thomas glanced at her list, clasped her brooch, and looked a little terrified.

"Lucida Sans."

Elaine watched Lucida get up from her seat and collect her spear and her broom horse and her helmet. "Good luck to you," she whispered.

There was a great deal of clanking and jangling as Lucida made her way past the eight students. She nearly fell into the aisle.

"Ouch, Lucida!"

"Watch your spear!"

Lucida made her way up the stairs at the side of the stage and drew aside the curtain at the edges. She turned to Ms. Thomas.

"I have taken the liberty of bringing my own musical accompaniment," Lucida told the music teacher as she kneeled down and blew some dust from an old record player. She plugged the turntable into the wall. From beneath her armor she produced an old record in a tattered sleeve.

"A vintage copy," she told the audience, "from Moms' basement." She clanked her way across the stage and took a spot directly at the center. She looked up at the ceiling and then back to the music teacher.

"Do we have any stage lights, Ms. Thomas?" she asked. "I do my best work in a spotlight." She lifted the front flap of her helmet and adjusted her fake goatee.

"I'm afraid not, Lucida," said Ms. Thomas from the bench. "This is just an audition. It will be a while before our stage crew hangs the lights."

"Oh, well. I guess I'll just begin, then."

Ms. Thomas's hand went to her brooch again. "Are you sure you don't want me to just play the piano?" she asked hopefully.

"Oh, no, Ms. Thomas. Like I said, I've brought the orchestration. I'll just sing along with that."

"Are you—are you quite sure?"

"Yes."

A few students in the front snickered, and someone shouted, "Where's your purple wig? You could wear it over your helmet!"

Lucida tilted her head back and held up the hinged flap so she could scan the audience.

"Who said that?" she yelled.

She tried to put her hands on her hips before shouting again, but she couldn't bend her arms properly in her armor. She fussed with her costume for a moment, but the right arm stuck straight out and she couldn't get the elbow joint to bend back down again. There was a great deal of creaking and banging and grunting.

"Would someone please help her get her arm down?" Ms. Thomas asked, looking anxiously out into the audience. The students laughed.

"I'll just make do," Lucida called, her arm still sticking out straight. Her voice was muffled behind the mask. "The show must go on."

Ms. Thomas said, "All right, Lucida." She looked tired.

Lucida walked back over to the record player just

behind the curtain and switched it on. She returned to the middle of the stage.

"I give you," she said, as the orchestration began, "'The Impossible Dream.'" She tapped her shoe and, counting to herself a few times, began to sing along with the scratchy recording.

"To dream the impossible dream
To fight the unbeatable foe
To bear with unbearable sorrow
To run where the brave dare not go"

Lucida lifted her good arm and walked to the left of the audience, which was stage right, and continued singing.

"To right the unrightable wrong
To love pure and chaste from afar"

And then, suddenly, just as Lucida was making her way back to center stage, the tempo of the song changed, slowly, unnoticeably, at first, but then slightly faster, then faster, and then so quickly that Lucida, looking terribly confused, struggled desperately to keep up with the record.

"Totrywhenyourarmsaretooowearytoreachtheunreach-
ablestar"

Next, just as quickly as the music hastened, it returned to normal speed for a moment before slowing down, at first gradually, then slower and slower, until the music was so slow that Lucida was forced to dance in slow motion while singing the words as if she were drunk, or perhaps had just been given an elephant tranquilizer.

"This . . . is . . . my . . . quest
To................ foll...................ow
that..................... staaaaaaaaaaaaaaaaaaaaaaar
No.............................. maaaaaaaaaaaaaaat-
ter how hhhhhhhhhhhhhhhhhopeless
No maaaaaaaaaaaaaaaaaaaaatter how
faaaaaaaaaaaaaaaaaaaaaaaaaaar"

Until the record sped up again and Lucida had to sing and dance as if her life depended upon it. Faster and slower the song went, with Lucida racing through the words in one moment, then dragging herself through them the next. From her seat, Elaine's heart raced, for of course she, along with all the other students in the auditorium, could see

Croton Harmon hovering over the record player, his fingers on the turntable. She considered telling Ms. Thomas, but she was wedged in a corner seat and would have to contend with eight pairs of knees again. She thought about shouting something from her seat and was just beginning to consider finding the courage to take a breath, when she looked up and saw that Croton Harmon, his hand still on the record, was looking out from behind the curtain, staring right at her. He scowled. Elaine looked at her shoes, knowing in that instant that poor Lucida was on her own, that she would never be brave enough to save her.

Meanwhile, Lucida looked out into the audience, took stock of Croton's empty seat, looked to the side of the stage behind the curtain, let out a scream, and charged stage right, her spear high over her head. There was a great deal of shuffling and struggling behind the curtain, the terrible sound of a needle scratching across a record, and then, finally, just as Ms. Thomas was about to rush the stage, Lucida appeared from behind the curtain once more. Most of the tinfoil had fallen off her costume, her broom-handle horse was missing its head, and her spear was bent in half. The helmet, though still on her head, was sideways, with the eyes looking off to the right. Her right arm was still sticking straight out.

“I would like,” Lucida said, pulling the helmet off with her left hand and smiling sweetly at the audience, “to finish my performance.” She turned to the curtain, screwed up her eyes, and hurled her helmet across the stage. Then she looked back at the audience and gave another sweet smile.

“Due to unforeseen circumstances,” she said, adjusting her wig, “I will be performing the remainder of this song a cappella.” She cleared her throat, licked her fingers, and ran them over her false goatee.

It is hard to describe the manner in which Lucida Sans made her way through the rest of “The Impossible Dream.” Suffice it to say that she did sing the remaining lines and verses, and she hit each note in perhaps not exactly the style in which it was intended, but ultimately, Elaine thought, in a very unique and satisfying way.

“This is my quest
To follow that star
No matter how hopeless
No matter how far”

Elaine leaned forward in her seat, and stray wisps of hair broke free from her ponytail and fell into her eyes. She smoothed the wisps back again, and lifted her head to the stage, and watched Lucida with great admiration. Lucida sang on.

"To fight for the right
Without question or pause
To be willing to march into Hell
For a heavenly cause"

And on. She sang each verse twice, perhaps to make up for lost time, and the last verse three times. Elaine shook her head and bit her lower lip until her eyes watered. She rested her clenched fists on her knees and leaned forward.

"And I know if I'll only be true
To this glorious quest
That my heart will lie peaceful and calm
When I'm laid to my rest

And the world will be better for this
That one man, scorned and covered with scars
Still strove with his last ounce of courage
To reach the unreachable star"

Lucida took off her wig and finished the last line of the song at a very high pitch, and she held the note for such a long time, and her face turned to such an unusual color, that the students fell silent in their seats and Ms. Thomas squeezed her brooch so hard it broke. A chill ran down Elaine's spine as she sat back in her seat, exhausted, her forehead beaded with perspiration. Lucida bowed deeply and clanked across the stage in the direction of the stairs. A stillness fell over the auditorium. Elaine stood up, clapped loudly, realized she was the only one applauding, and sat down again. Everyone in the row in front of her turned and stared. There was a long and uncomfortable silence.

"Well," Ms. Thomas said. "Well." She glanced at the front of her blouse, which was wrinkled from clutching her breast during Lucida's final note, and tried to smooth it down a little.

"Thank you for that . . . original version," she said. She sat down at the piano bench and closed her eyes.

Croton came out from behind the curtain. His shirt was torn and there was a piece of tinfoil in his hair. He returned to his seat.

"I'll get you back for this," Lucida screamed.

"Talent scouts!" Croton shouted back. "The festival was crawling with them!"

"You need me, Croton! Admit it to yourself!"

"Children, *please*," said Ms. Thomas, clutching her papers. "Croton, it's your turn, thank *goodness*. . . ."

The students began talking all at once. Elaine saw an opportunity to get up from her seat and hurry out of the auditorium. She was halfway down the hall toward the school's exit when Lucida, out of breath and quite flushed, finally caught up with her.

"Well, I guess I bombed another one," she said. "Thanks for coming, though."

"I—I must go. I have homework to do," Elaine lied.

"Well, wait up. I'll walk home with you."

"I am utilizing public transportation," Elaine said, resorting to the elevated language she always used when she was extremely nervous. "I have some errands to run."

"Public transport—oh, you mean the bus? What kind of errands? I could go with you."

"I'd rather you not."

Lucida looked surprised then, and a little hurt. They were standing at the front entrance of the school, at the top of the steps. Elaine, who had enjoyed enough public exposure for one day, began walking down the stairs.

"What's the matter with you?"

"Nothing."

Elaine continued walking down the street. Lucida, tripping over her foil-covered boots and stiff armor, struggled to keep up, her right arm still sticking straight out in the air.

"Was it Croton? That rotten fig. He got the better of me this time, but I'm going to get him back good, you'll see."

Elaine walked swiftly down the street.

"Did you—did you not like my performance?"

"No."

"You thought I was stupid, didn't you. But you were the only one who clapped. I don't get it."

"I did not think you were stupid."

"Stop for a second, will ya? I can't keep up with you in my chain mail."

Elaine stopped walking. They were a few blocks away from the school now, in front of a little empty playground.

"Sit down here a minute while I take off these boots," Lucida said. Elaine sighed, but she obeyed.

Lucida pulled herself out of her armor, kicked off her boots, and removed a makeup kit from her bag. She took out a jar of something that looked to Elaine like cooking oil, poured it onto a napkin, and began rubbing vigorously over her eyes. She removed her false mustache.

"Nobody liked it," Lucida said. "They all laughed."

"I did not laugh," Elaine said.

"Do you think I shouldn't have sung that last verse four times? I thought it gave the notes more clarity. Then again Moms always tell me that less is more."

Elaine thought this over.

"I don't know anything about it," she said finally. "I'm not familiar with the world of the stage."

"Well, you don't have to be familiar with the world of the stage to give me your honest opinion," Lucida said. She put down her horse and began to undo her chain mail.

Elaine thought hard for a moment. "Do all singing tryouts have a silent dance solo?" she asked.

"Not necessarily," Lucida said, and she looked like she was thinking this over. "But I thought I'd try something, you know—avant-garde."

"What year does the musical take place?"

"Around 1610."

"Did they have tap dance then?"

"Well, my interpretation was meant to show—"

"And the confetti?"

"—the joy of achievement, the triumph of success!" Lucida exploded angrily and stuffed her headpiece into her satchel. She took off her wig and began to walk away.

"Please don't take offense," said Elaine. Now it was her turn to follow behind Lucida.

"You're just like the rest of them, anyway. I was hoping you were different. But you were laughing like all of them."

"I certainly was not," said Elaine. "As you mentioned, I was the only one who clapped."

"Yes, but that was just to humor me," Lucida said. She wiped away a tear with her wig.

"That's a false accusation," Elaine said.

"Why should I believe you?"

"The words to that song," Elaine began, stopping on the path. She looked as though she were concentrating very hard. "The words made me feel so—"

"So what?" asked Lucida in earnest, turning her tear-streaked face to Elaine. They were standing at the bus stop now, and an old woman stood to one side, carrying four plastic bags filled with toilet paper and napkins. She looked at Lucida and moved away a little.

"I cannot express myself," Elaine said, feeling uncomfortable.

"No, tell me," said Lucida. "I'd really like to know. The words made you feel so—so what?"

"So—so confident, I suppose. Strong, maybe. As if, without the permission of others, I could be . . . as if I could be . . ." Elaine paused and looked at her shoes, nearly whispering the last few words, ". . . whatever I wanted."

"Well, that's what I'm talking about!" Lucida said, and she threw her arms around Elaine. The old woman standing at the other side of the bus stop stared.

"Oh, Elaine, I knew you would understand my interpretation of the song. I knew you believed in me!"

The bus arrived. It rumbled along the street and stopped in front of the old woman and the two girls. The door swung open, and the old woman fought to get up the steps with her parcels.

"I have to go," Elaine said, suddenly feeling quite spent. "My errands . . ."

Lucida beamed. "I'll call you tonight," she said. "We can talk more about this later."

But Elaine had talked more about herself—about something that was meaningful to her—than she ever had in her whole life. She felt so tired that she wasn't sure she would find the strength to strain *crêpe* batter when she got home. She followed the old woman up the steps, found her seat on the bus, and slumped into it.

Lucida grinned, waved at Elaine in the window, and lifted her spear above her head. Elaine looked away. The bus went on down the street.

5

"It's Croton's fault that I didn't even make the chorus," Lucida told Elaine a week or so later, as they sat in the cafeteria at the beginning of their lunch hour. It was Friday, and Lucida was dressed like a mouse. She stared down at the special of the day, a flat, pale tongue of meat called Supremely Steak, and jabbed at it with her fork.

"He made me lose my concentration," Lucida said. She separated her scalloped potatoes from one another and squirted ketchup from a plastic package in between each one. "I'm sure I would have gotten that solo if it weren't for him."

Elaine nodded. She took out a stack of plastic containers

and a square plate from her schoolbag and placed everything on the lunch table.

"What did you bring today?"

"Nothing special."

"Oh, sure."

Elaine unrolled a cloth napkin and took out her utensils. She was accustomed to eating by herself in a corner of the cafeteria where nobody paid attention to her, but since Lucida had decided to be her new friend, it was becoming increasingly difficult to eat alone.

"They have plastic forks and knives over by the soda machine, you know," Lucida said. "Along with condiments and plates."

"I prefer my own cutlery," Elaine said, arranging the napkin in her lap.

"I don't know why I allow Croton to get the best of me," Lucida said, touching the packing tape that held her mouse whiskers in place. "I'll get him, though. I'm devising a plan."

"You are?" asked Elaine. She opened one of the plastic containers, which had thin layers of smoked salmon in it.

"Yes," said Lucida. "To exact our revenge."

"*Our* revenge?"

Elaine removed a Wet-Nap from the outer pocket of

her bag and meticulously wiped her hands, pulling the cloth over each finger before discarding it on the edge of her tray. Then, with her fingers and her paring knife, she arranged the salmon on the plate so it looked like a rose.

"Yes. I have an idea, but I can't do it alone. I need your help." Lucida opened a packet of sugar and added it to the ketchup in between the scalloped potato slices. Elaine opened a small jar of capers and spooned a few over the salmon flower so they fell over the petals.

"Croton wants to be famous as much as I do," Lucida said. "He wants to be in everything. There's a big audition coming up that he won't tell anyone about because he's afraid of competition. But when I find out where it is, I am going to try out. And I am going to beat him so good he'll never forget it."

Elaine sliced a cucumber lengthwise into paper-thin sheets, stacked them on top of one another, and diced the mound into little cubes. She drizzled olive oil over the dice and added some feta-cheese squares from another container. She withdrew a baguette from her bag.

"How do you know there's an audition if only he knows about it?"

"He told me," Lucida said. "He called me on the phone and asked for my help, since I know a lot about costumery and scriptwriting and theater in general."

"What did you tell him?"

"I told him to forget it. That I'm tired of being used just for my experience. That's why I broke up with him in the first place."

"He didn't tell you anything about the audition? Like where it is or what it's for?"

Lucida shook her head.

"So what do you think of my plan to beat him at this audition?" Lucida asked.

Elaine sliced the baguette. "Well, I would need some time to think about it all," she said. "But if you are asking for my initial impression, I would have to say that I anticipate two problems. Maybe three."

"Go on," Lucida said.

"The first problem," Elaine said, "is the audition itself. You say he told you that an audition is coming up. But he didn't tell you anything else about it. How will you extract information from Croton that he's unwilling to provide?"

"Well—"

"And how do you plan to keep him from sabotaging future tryouts, even if you do beat him at this one?" Elaine tasted her salad and added freshly ground pepper. "I think you're probably attempting to achieve the unachievable."

She forked up some cucumber and a bit of salmon.

"What's the third thing?" Lucida asked, looking a little hurt.

"Pardon me?"

"You said there might be a third problem."

"There's no assurance you'll win the audition. What if it calls for the part of a man?"

"Oh, please," said Lucida. "If I can dress like a mouse, I can dress like a man."

Elaine nodded.

"Look," said Lucida, grabbing her fork and knife and sawing at her Supremely Steak with sudden ferocity. "Are you on my side or aren't you?" Unsuccessful at making a dent in her steak, she picked it up and began whacking it against the yellow lunch tray.

Elaine handed her a steak knife.

"Of course I'm on your side," Elaine replied. "I just don't understand the manner in which you plan on exacting this revenge."

Lucida cut her meat into many small pieces. She tasted a bit of the vegetable ensemble, a colony of dry baby carrots, soggy peas, and corn, and opened another package of sugar.

"Listen," she said, looking excited. "You don't understand Croton. He's terrible at keeping secrets. If we hover around him long enough, he'll mention the audition to somebody and we'll overhear it. As far as our revenge goes, I already have a plan worked out that will fix him forever."

"What's that?"

"One of Croton's secret wishes is to be a playwright. Being a singer or an actor isn't enough fame for him. He also dreams about starring in plays that he writes himself."

Elaine finished her salmon.

"He's terrible, too," Lucida went on. "His plays are the worst. Some of them don't even have any characters. He read pages to me when I used to be in love with him."

"Aren't you still in love with him?"

"Of course not! Now listen. Croton would never admit to this, but he's insecure about his plays. He types them up and sends them to theater companies in New York, hoping they'll write back and tell him how talented he is. So he can tell people how good he is at everything, see." Lucida leaned forward and pointed her mouse paw at Elaine. "And let me tell you something, Elaine. If you need to tell someone how good you are," she said. "You are probably not that good."

Elaine blinked.

"Here's my idea," Lucida said. "We get together and

write a fake letter from some theater people saying that they think his latest play is the boldest piece of writing since . . . since . . ."—Lucida squirted mayonnaise on her vegetable colony—"since Shakespeare."

"Shakespeare?"

"Okay, Sophocles. Trust me. He'll love it."

Elaine diced some chives on a plastic cutting board.

"So we send this phony letter," Lucida continued. "With letterhead from some fancy playhouse in the city. In the letter we tell him to show up somewhere all the kids hang out, like the Muddy Cup. I think the chess club meets there on Wednesdays, and those guys think Croton is an idiot. We specify that he must perform one of his monologues to see how it tests out. What do you think?"

Elaine pushed the chives off the knife with her thumb into a small container of whipped butter. "Then what?" she asked.

"Then nothing," Lucida said. "He dresses up like a tree or a garden hose. People laugh, he gets embarrassed. Later we'll write him a note explaining that if he wrecks Lucida's audition again, the revenge will go on and on, taking different forms."

Elaine put down her knife.

"Wouldn't it be much easier to apologize for ruining

Romeo and Juliet at Festival on the Green and be done with it?" she asked. "All these revenge acts. It's hard enough just to get through high school."

Lucida ate an enormous spoonful of vegetables with ketchup, mayonnaise, and sugar. She chewed a bite of Supremely Steak about three hundred times.

"First of all, what happened at *Romeo and Juliet*," Lucida said, pointing her fork, "was not my fault."

"Yes, but—"

Lucida held up her mouse paw.

"Second, Croton will never forgive me. Even if I do apologize."

"Why not?"

Lucida wrapped up the leftover bites of Supremely Steak in a paper towel and stuffed it into the pocket of her mouse costume.

"Because he's a sociopath," she said, wiping her face with a paper napkin. "A histrionic, narcissistic borderline splitter, as listed in the *Diagnostic and Statistical Manual of Mental Disorders*."

Lucida scraped up the rest of her vegetables and pushed them into a paper cup. She shrugged.

"Like I said, he's a rotten fig. A flower gone to seed. It's a sorry truth, Elaine, but the only way to beat Croton

Harmon is to prove you are more powerful. Or else you get squashed."

"I'm not familiar with the *Diagnostic and Statistical Manual of Mental Disorders*," said Elaine, spreading a slice of bread with chive butter and handing it to Lucida. She began putting her plastic containers together and rolling her utensils back into the cloth napkin. She returned everything to her schoolbag.

"We have to beat him at his own game," Lucida said. She snapped closed her mouse purse, which had a tail. "It's that simple. Now, are you with me or aren't you?"

"I don't understand how you need my help, Lucida."

"I need you to help me write the letter, silly. I'm not as good a writer as you."

"How do you know I'm such a good writer?"

"Anyone who uses words like 'inquiry' instead of just plain 'ask' has got to be a decent writer," Lucida said. "Besides, that's not the only part I need help with."

Elaine looked at Lucida.

"I need you to sneak into Croton's bedroom with me."

"What?"

"To get the list. Of theaters. I don't know where he sends his stupid plays. He keeps the names and addresses in a drawer."

"I will not sneak into anyone's bedroom."

"Oh, come on, Elaine," said Lucida as they gathered their things together.

"I cannot."

"Where's your adventure?"

"No. Please find someone else, Lucida. I'm not the kind of person who takes dangerous chances. I can't—"

At that moment Croton Harmon came into the cafeteria. He moved quickly, looking around to make sure that no one was watching him make his way to the lunch table where Lucida and Elaine were having their conversation. Lucida picked up her tray as soon as she saw him. "Come on, Elaine," she said. "Let's go."

Elaine froze in her seat, terrified at the sight of the rotten fig himself.

Croton moved between Lucida and the trash receptacle.

"Nice outfit," he said. "Who are you playing today?"

"Mickey Mouse," said Lucida, trying to brush past him. "Leave us alone."

"You don't look like Mickey Mouse," said Croton, pulling Lucida's tail and pulling her backward. "You look like a regular mouse."

"It was before he got discovered," Lucida replied. "Come on, Elaine."

"No, wait. I want to tell you something." Croton looked around the cafeteria again.

"What?"

"I just wanted to say," said Croton, moving closer and putting his hands on Lucida's mouse shoulders. "I'm really sorry you lost that audition."

"Where's your entourage?" said Lucida, shrugging Croton's hands away. "You wouldn't even be talking to me if any of your lackeys were around."

"I thought you were really good."

"If it weren't for you, I'd have gotten that solo."

"I gave you an opportunity to improvise. Even Ms. Thomas agreed after I talked to her. She said she was going to change her mind. She says she wants you to be in the chorus."

Lucida turned around. Her face softened a little.

"Really?" she asked. "Ms. Thomas said that?"

"Yes," said Croton. He winked at Elaine, who looked down at her shoes.

"Well, that was—that was nice of you, Croton," said Lucida.

"Listen," Croton said, lowering his voice. "What do you say we just call it a truce, all right? You got me at the Festival on the Green, and I got you at auditions last week." His voice dropped another decibel. "What say we get back together again? You don't need to hang around with girls like her." He pointed with his chin at Elaine, still frozen at the cafeteria bench, clenching her schoolbag.

"She's my new friend," Lucida said.

"I need you," Croton said.

"I'm not falling for this again," said Lucida. "You're a rotten fig, a flower gone to seed. You're a histrionic, narcissistic borderline splitter."

"Maybe," Croton said, and his voice was still so low that Elaine could barely hear him. He ducked his head at Lucida and offered a hopeful smile, showing his irresistible dimples. "C'mon, Lucie, give me another chance."

"I don't know, Croton," Lucida said hesitantly. "You never let me go around with any of your friends."

"I'll tell them how special you are."

"When?"

"Eventually. It's just, you know"—and then he lowered his voice to a near whisper—"I have this reputation, you understand." He stared into her eyes. Lucida softened.

Don't you do it, Lucida, thought Elaine. He's a rotten fig. He's a flower gone to seed.

"Just give me a little time. A few weeks to get my friends to warm up to you."

"But I waited and waited," Lucida said, her face opening up like a rosebud.

Oh, no, Elaine thought.

Croton pulled off Lucida's mouse hood and started to remove her whiskers, one by one, from beneath the packing tape. He removed them gingerly, looking down at Lucida with love. Or at least to Lucida it looked like love. To Elaine, watching from beyond the trash receptacle, it looked more like self-love. To Elaine, looking into Croton's cold, black eye was like staring into the window of a collection of pathologies, all carefully listed and categorized in the *Diagnostic and Statistical Manual of Mental Disorders*.

"Just give me some time," whispered Croton. He pressed Lucida's face into his chest. "A few days. I haven't told them how much I need you, but I do, I swear."

Lucida looked into Croton's face, her eyes large and childlike.

"Really, Croton?" Lucida squeaked, like a real mouse. "Truly?"

The cafeteria door swung open on the other side of the cafeteria. Six of Croton's friends from the previous week's audition entered the room. They moved in strange unison, like a small army, approaching and then surrounding the lunch table where Lucida and Croton were having their conversation.

"What's this about?" a redheaded girl asked as a few blond-haired boys stared at Elaine.

"Nothing," said Croton, and to avoid looking like he had been hanging around with Lucida, he shoved her away from him so abruptly that she fell backward into someone carrying a lunch tray. There was a loud crash, and Lucida found herself on the floor, covered from whiskers to tail in peas and carrots, Supremely Steak, and red Jell-O. Globs of coagulated gelatin ran down her hair and into her face. There was a burst of laughter and a large round of applause.

Lucida got up. She shook the peas and carrots out of her hair and removed a cube of Jell-O hanging from the end of one of her whiskers.

Croton stepped away. "Let's go," he said to one of the blond-haired boys. The group moved away together, still in unison, in the direction of the exit. Elaine could see them talking and laughing as they went through the swinging door.

Lucida got up and took a deep breath. She straightened her shoulders.

"Forget him!" shouted a boy on the chess team, from the other side of the cafeteria.

"Yeah, Lucida, you deserve better!"

"He's a rotten fig!" a girl in braces shrieked.

"A flower gone to seed!"

"I fall for it every time," Lucida whispered. "Because he's so handsome. He's my weakness."

Elaine picked up Lucida's hood and mouse purse with the tail. She collected a few of Lucida's whiskers that had fallen on the floor and rolled them into a napkin. When she straightened up, Lucida was staring at her, biting her lip, looking pleadingly into her eyes.

"Oh, all right," Elaine said finally. She shrugged. "Let us avenge."

Dear Julia,

I am starting to believe that I lack bravery. In your book *Mastering the Art of French Cooking, Volume I*, you noted that loosening eggs from a pan requires courage.

For a while I believed that the problem with the omelette was that I was not tilting the pan at an even, 20-degree angle over the heat. But today I came to the realization that perhaps the problem is not with the heat or the angle, or even a matter of forcing the egg mass to roll over on itself.

Maybe the problem has more to do with courage.

Sincerely,

Elaine Hamilton

6

"We need to open the letter with a real bang," Lucida said to Elaine as she followed her up and down the aisles of Paltz Produce & Co., the specialty market on the far side of town. Elaine had refused to stay after school to help Lucida write her phony letter because it was Friday, and Elaine always prepared an elaborate meal on Fridays. Lucida, dressed as an artist, hurried to keep up with Elaine in the aisles of the crowded market, clutching her paintbrush and palette in one hand, her schoolbags and pencil in the other. People wheeled by with their grocery carts and stared. Elaine navigated her cart toward the root vegetables, too busy to notice Lucida's engine red tights, her plaid skirt, the black wig beneath her red beret.

"Do you always do the shopping for your whole family?" Lucida asked as Elaine inspected an onion.

"Usually," Elaine said. Elaine did not tell Lucida that the evening's dinner menu included Rôti de Boeuf Poêlé à la Matignon with braised carrots and green beans, Gratin Dauphinois, and a Riz à l'Impératrice for dessert. Fortunately, Lucida was too caught up in her revenge letter to ask any other questions. She laid a sheet of notebook paper over her palette and, adjusting her paintbrush behind her right ear, followed Elaine down the narrow aisles of the supermarket like a summer camp director holding a clipboard.

"'Dear Croton,'" she began. "No, wait." She turned the pencil over and erased furiously. "'Dear Sir,'" she said. She squinted at the paper. "No, that's too formal." She erased again.

Elaine sorted through a pile of carrots until she found the ones she liked. She filled a bag and put it on the scale. She looked at the dial and added a few more.

"What's his last name?" Elaine asked as Lucida followed her to the potato bin.

"Harmon."

"Dear Mr. Harmon," Elaine said, holding up a potato

and looking at it in the light. It seemed to pass her inspection, so she ripped off a plastic bag and put the potato inside.

"Ooh, you're good," said Lucida. She scribbled the words on the notebook paper. "Congratulations,'" she said, talking as she wrote. "You're the best playwright in the world. We want to try and produce your play and make you a rich—"

"That's too effusive," said Elaine, weighing the potatoes. "You need to sound more restrained."

"Oh, right, restrained," Lucida repeated. She turned the pencil over again and erased. She looked puzzled. "What do you mean, restrained?"

"Dear Mr. Harmon," said Elaine, pushing her grocery cart past fennel and lovage on the way to the cheese counter. "We are writing to inform you that we have read your play and found yours to be quite a fresh and original new voice."

"Wait, wait," Lucida said, her pencil passing across the palette furiously. "Fresh and original new voice," she murmured, dotting the end of the sentence.

"And we would very much like to"—Elaine squinted at the white labels beneath the packages of neatly wrapped cheese—"to . . ." She turned to Lucida.

"What do theaters do with plays, anyway?" she asked.

"They try to find sponsors," Lucida answered. "They find rich people to put up money so they can produce their shows. You know, like for Broadway."

Elaine did not know, but she shrugged her shoulders and turned back to the cheese. A heavy woman in a white apron smiled from behind the counter.

"Hey there, Elaine. How are you doing?"

"Fine, thank you," Elaine replied. "I see you have the *Pérail de brebis* today."

"Sure enough," the woman answered. "*Saint-Marcellin*, too," she added, handing both Lucida and Elaine a sample.

"Nice finish," Elaine said, nodding at the woman.

"Yech," said Lucida, making a face. "It tastes like grass."

"I'll take three quarters of a pound," said Elaine.

"Like sheep," Lucida said.

"Will that be all?" the woman asked, passing over the cheese in blue-and-white paper.

"How does she know you?" Lucida whispered.

"I also need a chunk of *Gruyère*. Do you have raw milk?"

"Certainly. We're getting some wonderful *Beaufort* next week, Elaine. Be sure to stop by."

"I will. Thank you."

"Now what do I say?" Lucida asked, after she had spit out her sample in the trash and hurried to catch up to Elaine.

"I guess, 'And we would very much like to find the appropriate sponsors to produce your play . . .'" Elaine picked up a jar of glacéed fruit. "What's the play called, anyway?"

"I don't know. We'll fill that in after we sneak into his bedroom."

Elaine sighed. "Then just put, 'And we would very much like to find the appropriate sponsors to produce your play' for now. Then put 'sincerely.' And write the name of the theater company. And that's it." Elaine counted out three more jars of fruit and placed them in her cart.

"Wait a second," Lucida said, running behind again as Elaine walked by the dairy section. "That can't be it. We have to add in the revenge part."

"You write that. I don't want to be involved."

"Are you forgetting that he humiliated me in front of everyone? How would you feel if he had done that to you?"

Elaine shivered, only partly because she was standing in front of the refrigerated dairy section. She would have hated it if someone had embarrassed her in front of everyone. She picked up a carton of heavy cream and held it to her chest.

"Oh, all right." She pushed the cart away from Lucida

again, this time in the direction of the meat counter. She didn't stop until she had reached the other side of the market. A man in a white butcher's coat smiled when he saw Elaine approaching the counter.

"Hi, Elaine. What can I do for you this week?"

"You know him, too?" said Lucida.

"Hi, Rusty," she said. "Any prime *filet* today?"

"No prime," he answered. "But I've got some wonderful grass fed. Want to have a look?"

"If you don't mind."

Rusty removed a hunk of meat from behind the glass and sheared a piece off with his butcher's knife. He placed it on a piece of waxed paper and presented it to Elaine. Elaine examined the meat, poked it a little with her finger, smelled it, even stretched it a little.

"Hmm. Do you have about five pounds?"

"Four and a half, maybe."

"Four and a half is okay. I'd like it trimmed, please."

"Sure thing, Elaine."

"I need a piece of suet, too. About four inches wide." She held her thumb and index finger apart.

"How much you want?"

"The length of the *filet*."

The butcher cut and wrapped Elaine's meat in stiff

white paper. He handed it to her in a plastic bag over the top of the counter.

"Be sure to give my best to your mother."

"I will."

"Eww, why does your mother tell you to smell the meat?" Lucida asked as Elaine walked down the beverage aisle. "And where's your list, anyway? You got all these things memorized?"

"We would like to help you in your search for the appropriate sponsors," Elaine continued, ignoring Lucida's questions. Lucida picked up her pencil again. "But unfortunately, timely as your play seems, we are not yet convinced your story will translate to the stage. In the interest of the theater, then, we are making a small request that you first perform a segment of the show for unspecified viewers. We realize this may seem atypical, but be assured that this is a new method of selection, modern and avant-garde as it may sound."

Lucida's pencil was a blur as she scribbled the words across the page.

"Oh, man, this is great," she said.

"Please prepare as you would for a real performance—"

Lucida scrawled like a madwoman.

" . . . and show up in full costume at— Where did you say you want him to show up?" Elaine asked.

"The Muddy Cup," said Lucida. "Definitely there. And let's make it for two thirty, right after school, on a Wednesday, because that's when the chess club and all those freshmen hang out after school. Croton knows they think he's a talentless phoney."

"All right," said Elaine.

"And I'll add that he should just come into the café, stand on top of a table, and deliver one of his dumb soliloquies."

"Yes, and don't use the word 'dumb,'" said Elaine. "And don't forget to mention the talent scout will be there. So he'll do his best."

Lucida put the finishing touches on her letter as Elaine hurried around the store, picking up celery and onions and parsley sprigs. By now Elaine's cart was nearly filled to the top. She headed toward the checkout aisle.

"Okay, so, I'll see you tonight?" Lucida stuffed the notebook paper into her bag and removed the paint-brush from behind her ear. She tugged at her skirt and adjusted her wig.

"What?"

"We have to sneak into Croton's house. But don't

worry. He always goes to the movies with those self-impressed fakers from school."

"I'm not going through anyone's bedroom window—"

"Who said anything about a bedroom window?" Lucida replied as they moved down closer to the register. "I happen to be an excellent lock picker. There isn't any lock in town that two bobby pins and a paper clip can't fix."

"And what about his parents?" Elaine asked. "Will they also be at the cinema?"

"No," Lucida said, looking as though she hadn't considered this. "Come to think of it, they're always home. But they just watch television in the den. We'll sneak right by them."

"I don't have a good feeling," Elaine said, lifting the onions out of the cart. "I don't have a good feeling about this at all."

"Well, I have a great feeling about it," Lucida said, taking the carrots out of the cart and placing them on the conveyer belt. The cashier stared at Lucida for a moment, shrugged, and popped a huge pink bubble of gum. "I have an amazing feeling about it!" Lucida nearly shouted, hurrying to unload the cart. "I can hardly wait!"

Elaine got home from Paltz Produce & Co. at around four o'clock, an hour behind schedule. She had hoped she would get home before her two oldest brothers, but she could already hear Francis bouncing his basketball on the washing machine and Chris shouting at him to cut it out. She carried her bags through the hall and into the kitchen, where she checked each item against the receipt to make sure everything was there. Then she went over to the shelf and took down *Mastering the Art of French Cooking, Volume Two*. She opened to the correct page. She knew all the recipes by heart, of course, but she liked to look at the pages to reassure herself. She went to the sink and scrubbed her hands. She put on her apron.

"Quit doing that," Chris cried from the other room. "You're going to break the washing machine. It's a triple loader."

"Mind your business," said Francis.

The twins, Robyn and Leslie, wandered into the kitchen. They were hard to tell apart.

"Eeelaynee," Robyn said. "What are you making for dinner?"

"Rôti de Boeuf Poêlé à la Matignon," said Elaine. "With braised carrots and green beans."

"Are we helping?" asked Leslie.

"Of course," said Elaine. "You can wash carrots. Les will do the onions."

The twins pulled two kitchen chairs out from under the table and dragged them over to the counter. They set to work on the vegetables, removing each one from the bag with their small hands and dropping them into the sink.

"Elaynee," said Leslie, peeling an onion. "Chris went in your closet today."

"He tried on a skirt," Robyn said.

"*And* your earrings," Leslie added.

Elaine nodded. "Wash the carrots well. They're root vegetables and might have residual particles of soil." She took out a jar of glacéed fruit and held it up in front of her brothers.

"These are fruits such as cherries, orange peel, citron, apricots, and angelica, which have   "

"   undergone a preservation process—" Robyn continued.

"—in sugar," finished Leslie.

"Correct," said Elaine. "Now watch the way I prepare the dessert mixture." She mixed the fruit in a bowl with a few tablespoons of cognac and sprinkled gelatin over the top.

"I'll set the bowl aside in order to prepare the rice," she said. "Robyn, are the carrots scrubbed?"

"Yes."

"Let's wash the potatoes and begin slicing for the Gratin Dauphinois. As usual, keep a firm grip. Let the knife do the work for you."

"Francis, cut it *out*," Chris shrieked.

"Hey, give that back! Give it back!" There was a thundering of feet in the hall.

Elaine's third oldest brother, Lynn, wandered into the kitchen wearing tights and a bodysuit. He was chubby and filled his suit like a little dumpling. He squinted in the light of the kitchen.

"What's for supper?" he asked.

"Roti de Boeuf Poêlé à la Matignon," said Leslie.

"And grawteen dafinoys," said Robyn.

"Gratin Dauphinois," corrected Lynn as Leslie peeled and Robyn sliced. "A French-inspired potato dish, from the obsolete *grater*, to scratch, or to scrape, the gratin is a top crust of browned crumbs and butter, often with grated cheese."

"When are the regionals?" Elaine asked, adjusting Robyn's grip on the knife handle.

"Two weeks," said Lynn.

"Lynn, are you in the kitchen?" a voice from the basement called.

"Yes," Lynn called back. "*Dauphinois*," he said. "*D-a-u-p-h-i-n-o-i-s*."

"Come on. Let's purify." A slow chant came up from the basement. *"Ohmm. Ohmm. Ohmm. Asatho Maa Sath Gamayaaaah."*

Lynn shrugged helplessly and trudged down the stairs to the basement.

"*Thamaso Maa Jyothir Gamaya*."

"Dry the beef thoroughly on paper towels," Elaine told Leslie. "And I'll demonstrate the proper tying method."

Elaine was removing butter from the refrigerator when Francis chased Chris into the kitchen. Francis was wearing a hockey jersey. Chris was wearing Elaine's pink furry slippers and her favorite yellow nightgown. He hugged the basketball to his chest and screamed when Francis tried to pry it from his arms.

"Give it *back*."

"Not unless you promise to quit hitting me."

"Don't be such a baby. I was kidding around."

Elaine unwound some butcher's string. "I don't mind your wearing my slippers," she told Chris, "but that is my favorite nightgown."

"Give it back," Francis demanded, swiping the air at Chris. He lunged and dove, and Chris covered his eyes.

"Not without a promise!" he shrieked, going down.

"*Asatho Maa Sath Gamayaaaah,*" came the chant from the basement. "*Thamaso Maa Jyothir Gamaya*."

"That's it. Feel your breath, Lynn. Do you feel it?"

Francis pinned Chris to the kitchen floor. Chris kicked the furry slippers, which knocked over the chair holding one of the twins, who fell, bringing with him some onions and several sliced potatoes. He got up, righted the chair, and returned to the potatoes.

Chris and Francis rolled on the floor in onion peels.

"Elaynee, make them stop," said Robyn.

"My nightgown," said Elaine, slicing the butter, "is getting sullied."

"What's sullied?"

"*Ohm . . . Ohm . . . Ohm . . .* that's it, Lynn. Breathe through your nose. Breathe into it. See if you can get your leg up a tiny bit more."

Chris kicked Francis, and he flew across the kitchen floor, hitting the cabinet with a bang. Francis grinned and rubbed the back of his head.

"Nice legwork," he said.

Chris got up and straightened his nightgown. "Brute,"

he said. He leaned over the stove and sniffed. "What's for supper?" he asked.

"Did you peel the carrots?" Elaine asked Leslie.

Francis bounced the basketball against Chris's head. Chris smacked Francis, who knocked Robyn in the ribs. Robyn started to cry.

"Now look what you did," Chris yelled. He picked up Robyn and wiped his nose with a paper towel.

Elaine put down the butter to tend to the *filet*. It was soft and earthy and smelled wonderful. She patted it gently and tied it into a perfect cylinder. She poured one-eighth of an inch of oil in the bottom of a pan and set the heat on high. She browned the beef on all sides and on its two ends.

"Because I *can't*," came a cry from downstairs in the basement. There was a slapping of bare feet on the stairs.

"Quit it!" Chris said.

"Make me," said Francis.

"*Thamaso Maa Jyothir Gamaya*. Hey, come back here!"

Lynn appeared from the basement. There was a large rip in the seat of his bodysuit.

Francis said, "Look at Lynn's bodysuit, everybody."

"Leave him alone," Chris said. "Why don't you get out of the kitchen?"

"Elaynee, Chris smacked me," cried Robyn.

"I didn't smack you! That was Francis!"

"Now what do I do with the carrots?" asked Leslie.

"Put me down," said Robyn.

"Let me wipe your nose. It's still running."

"No, it's not."

Elaine laid the suet across the length of the *filet*. She spooned some oil out of the pan.

"Elaynee!"

"Cut it out!"

"Chris, you are sullying my nightgown," Elaine said.

"Sully. From the French, *souiller*. To soil or stain. S-u-l-l-y."

"Know-it-all!"

"Shut up!"

"You shut up!"

"Lynn, get down here *immediately*!"

Elaine set four quarts of water to boil for the Riz à l'Imperatrice.

"Stop touching me!"

"You touched me first!"

"No, I didn't!"

"Yes, you did!"

At six o'clock that same evening, Elaine served Céleri-Rave Rémoulade and a Mousse de Foies de Volaille as a first course.

"What's the mushy stuff?" Francis asked when everyone sat down at the table as Elaine served the hors d'oeuvres.

Elaine's mother, home from Washington, glanced up from the pages of her book, *Deliberative Democracy*, and surveyed the table.

"Looks like a *pâté*. It's a *pâté,* right, Elaine?"

"Mousse," Elaine answered. "Of chicken livers."

"Gross," said Lynn.

"Disgusting," said Francis.

"Delicious, Elaine," said their father, who was sitting between Robyn and Leslie. He spread some more on a cracker. "Simply delicious. Elizabeth, you must try some."

"Yes, yes," said Mrs. Hamilton, still looking at her book. She mumbled to herself and turned another page.

"Why can't we ever have spaghetti or meat loaf?" asked Francis. "Like normal families."

"Because we're not a normal family!" Chris sang, forking up another mouthful of celeriac in mustard sauce. He was still wearing Elaine's yellow nightgown.

"I don't want any," said Lynn.

"Me neither," said Francis.

"You have to at least try it," said their father. "It's divine. Here, boys, let me spread you some. You, too, Leslie."

"Dad, can I go out after dinner?" Francis asked.

"Where?"

"Drew and Terry want to play basketball later."

"What about homework?"

"I'll do it tomorrow."

"Ask your mother."

"Mom, can I?"

"I'm going to deflate that stupid basketball with one

of Elaine's skewers," said Chris, spreading another cracker thickly with mousse. "He hit me on the head with it. And just look at the bruises on my arms! I won't be able to go sleeveless for months."

Elaine's father frowned. "Let me see that arm," he said.

Francis scowled at Chris.

"I don't see any marks," said Mr. Hamilton.

"Mom, can I go?"

"What's this about?" Elaine's mother asked, looking up from her book and taking a bit of mousse and spreading it on a cracker. Elaine watched as her mother took a small bite and put it back on her plate.

"Francis wants to have a game with the boys after dinner," said Mr. Hamilton.

"Oh, I don't think so."

"Aw, crap."

"*Oooh*," Robyn and Leslie said at the same time, their mouths full of mousse.

"Jinx," Lynn said.

"Jinx what?" asked Chris.

"They said 'ooh' at the same time," Lynn explained. "Now they have to say 'jinx' and count to ten. Whoever gets to ten first is the winner."

"Jinx!" cried Leslie. "One-two-three-four-five-six-seven-eight-nine-ten. I win!"

"What does the winner get?" Chris asked.

"No fair, I wasn't ready," said Robyn.

"Come on, Mom, please."

"Not a chance, Francis. I spoke to Mr. Ivers the other day at the Society Benefit. He said you received a seventy-two percent on the chemistry quiz."

"Shit," said Francis.

"*Oooh*," Robyn and Leslie said at the same time, their mouths full of remoulade.

"Jinx," said Robyn. "One-two-three-four-five-six-seven-eight-nine-ten. What'd I win?"

"S-h-i-t," said Lynn. "In Middle English, *shiten*, a slang, often used to express disgust or frustration—"

"Lynn, that's enough," said Mr. Hamilton.

Robyn said, "I said jinx first."

Leslie said, "No, I did."

"No, I did."

"No, I—"

"Boys, *please*."

"What the hell is wrong with a seventy-two percent?" Francis demanded to know. He poked at his *rémoulade*. "Why does everyone have to be such a goddamn overachiever in this house? I hate chemistry."

"You could release the tension," Mr. Hamilton said, "with some chants and some breathing. Want to join me after dinner, Francis?"

"No, thanks!"

"I got a hundred on my history test, Dad," said Lynn.

"Well, how about that! Did you hear that, Elizabeth? Lynn got a hundred on his history test."

Francis kicked Lynn under the table.

"Francis kicked me!"

"Francis, try to set an example," said Mrs. Hamilton. She laid down her book on the table. "Elaine, is there anything to drink besides the Bordeaux? You didn't buy this yourself at Wine Sellers, did you?"

"I bought it," said Mr. Hamilton. He winked at Elaine. "Under Elaine's direction, of course."

"The boys shouldn't be having wine with dinner. Where's the milk?"

Elaine went to the refrigerator and took out a carton of milk. She looked at her *filet* surrounded by its vegetable, the trussing strings removed. She poured a few spoonfuls of sauce over the top and adjusted a few carrots and string beans, which were glazed to a shiny perfection. She took the Gratin Dauphinois out from the upper rack of the oven and placed it on the table. The cheese was brown and sizzling at the top, bubbling; beneath, the potatoes glistened in neatly layered rows.

"What were some of the questions on the history test?" Mrs. Hamilton asked Lynn.

"What was the date of the American Revolution? Who led the Boston Tea Party?"

Francis sulked.

"I'm hungry!" Leslie cried. "I want dafinoys."

"I want some carrots," said Robyn. "I sliced them on the bias."

"I want a nightgown like Elaine's," said Chris. "With that frill around the edges and the high neckline."

"Wait until you're thirteen," Francis told Lynn. "You get all the breaks until you hit seventh grade."

"Oh my, Elaine," said Mr. Hamilton as Elaine brought the platter to the table.

"Was that pork fat on top of the meat?" Mrs. Hamilton asked, putting down her book again and looking at the roast. She wrinkled her nose. "We'll all suffer heart attacks."

"Delicious, Elaine," said Mr. Hamilton, beginning to slice the *filet*. "Just delicious."

"Pass the potatoes," said Chris.

"Elaine, you're not touching your food," said Mr. Hamilton.

"I want a hamburger," said Francis.

"Me, too," said Lynn.

"If no one raises an objection," Elaine said stiffly, removing her apron, "I would like to leave early this evening."

Everyone stopped talking and eating and looked over. She cleared her throat.

"I realize that it's somewhat—somewhat irregular for me to interrupt our evening meal, but I—I have an engagement."

Mrs. Hamilton took a sip of water from her glass. She smiled a little.

"Are you going to see your new friend again?" Chris asked.

"Lucida Sans," said Mr. Hamilton dreamily, taking another bite of his *filet*. "Maybe we could invite Lucida Sans to dinner one night."

"Unfortunately I will be late for my engagement unless I leave in a timely manner," Elaine said.

"Where does she live, Elaine?" asked Mrs. Hamilton.

Elaine told her mother where Lucida lived and expressed that walking was her preferred mode of transportation.

"Did you let her walk all that way by herself, Edward? Why didn't you tell her to take the car?"

"Really, there is no need—"

"Oh, for goodness sake," Mrs. Hamilton said, and wiped her mouth with her napkin. She pushed out her chair.

"Go change. I'll wait for you in the car."

Elaine sat quietly in the passenger's seat as her mother drove down Front Street and made a right turn on Main.

"I'm so glad you've made a friend," she said, putting her hand on Elaine's pant leg for a moment before putting it back on the steering wheel. "I was afraid you were never going to leave the kitchen."

"I like the kitchen," Elaine said quietly.

"Yes, well, a social life is important, too, you know, Elaine. You need a range of experience out of the classroom, beyond academic pursuits. College admissions boards like to know you have an active social life in addition to high scores."

Elaine looked out the window.

"Yes," said Mrs. Hamilton, even though Elaine had not asked a question. She looked behind her in the rearview mirror. "A mind like yours, Elaine—a mind like yours doesn't belong in a hot kitchen with saucepans and casseroles. You could be whatever you want."

I want to be a chef, Elaine thought.

"I want you to have choices. You are my first child. My only daughter." She switched on her blinker and took a left on Chestnut, by the grocery store and the gas station.

"What did you say your friend's name was? Lucida? It's such an unusual name. And yet somehow I feel like I've heard it before."

Elaine pressed her forehead against the window.

"What are you two planning to do this evening?"

"I have to—we're going to—she wants me to help her write a letter."

"Something for school? Well, you're a wonderful writer. No wonder she wants your help."

Elaine thought it best not to tell her mother that she and Lucida were breaking into Croton Harmon's house to find out where he sent his terrible plays as part of an elaborate and complicated revenge plot.

Mrs. Hamilton turned onto Lucida's street. She looked out of the car at the little white house with brown trim.

"Will you stay over? You're welcome to, you know. Or maybe you could invite Lucida back here and have a sleepover at our house. I'm so glad you're coming out of your shell, Elaine."

The front door opened and Lucida ran across the lawn. She was dressed like a cat burglar, with a black shirt and pants and black nylon gloves. She wore a knit cap and a mask, and there was a flashlight attached to her belt. She crouched down low and held out her arms in front of her, darting back and forth across the yard to the driveway.

"She certainly looks like an interesting girl," said Mrs. Hamilton.

Elaine clapped a hand over her mouth and tried not to laugh.

"I should just say hello—"

"There's no need," said Elaine, pushing open the car door and stepping out. She waved good-bye to her mother as Lucida came down the front walk. She leaned into the open window on the passenger side.

"Hi, Mrs. Hamilton. I'm Lucida Sans."

"Why, hello, Lucida. It's—it's lovely to meet you. And may I say that is quite an interesting outfit."

"Really, we have to be leaving now," Elaine said, taking Lucida's arm and trying to pull her back up the front walk.

"Would you like to come in, Mrs. Hamilton? Moms would love to meet you. You are their absolute hero!"

"No, really—I—you girls have fun. I've got to get home to the boys."

Mrs. Hamilton drove off.

"Your mother wears quite a lot of lipstick," Lucida said, nodding approvingly after the car as it pulled away.

"And hair spray," said Elaine. "You should see how much hair spray she has."

"Well, she's lucky she's famous, that's all I have to say," said Lucida. "Now come on—let me show you the outfit I have picked out for you tonight. We're going to look spectacular! No one will even notice us!"

Elaine followed Lucida up her front walk and into the little house with the brown trim. She felt happy.

8

"I have a mask for you, too," Lucida said to Elaine after they had greeted the Moms and Lucida had pushed the feather boas, the scarves and lipsticks, a pair of vinyl pants, a corduroy necktie, a gold lamé shirt with rhinestones, and a prosthetic nose off her chenille bedspread.

"Oh, I couldn't," said Elaine.

"It was nothing. I got them two for one at Winette's Costumery."

"No, I mean—I can't. I will not wear a burglar mask."

"How come?" asked Lucida.

"It—it's not in my character," said Elaine.

"Oh, come on, where's your adventure?"

"No, thanks."

Lucida looked deflated.

Elaine sighed and removed her eyeglasses. She took the mask from Lucida. Since she couldn't see without her eyewear, she placed it over the mask. Lucida brought over a mirror, and they studied their reflections together.

"It's a nicer effect without the glasses, of course," said Lucida, tilting her head to one side. "But it still looks pretty good."

The girls looked at each other in their masks.

"It's fun to dress up, isn't it?" said Lucida. "Gives you a chance to imagine what it would be like to be somebody else."

Elaine, who had a hard enough time being herself, could not possibly imagine what it would be like to be someone else.

"I suppose," she said finally.

"Ready to go?"

"No."

"All right, then!"

Lucida threw open the door to her bedroom, and the girls walked down the hallway toward the front of the house, where Mrs. Fischburger Number One and Mrs. Fischburger Number Two were sitting in the living room reading papers together, their briefcases open, the coffee table littered with diet soda cans and take-out boxes of Chinese food.

"Going out, Isadora?" Mrs. Fischburger Number One asked. Neither looked up from their papers.

"Yup."

"Need the car?"

"Nope."

"All right," said Mrs. Fischburger Number Two. She glanced up from her briefs, squinted at the girls, and looked back at her papers. "Be careful. Don't walk through the park."

"We won't."

The girls opened the front door.

"Sue, were the girls wearing masks?" Elaine heard one of the Fischburger mothers ask as Lucida shut the front door and dashed across the lawn.

"Crouch! Crouch!" Lucida called behind her as they took a left on Hasbrouck and turned onto Chestnut.

"I will not crouch."

"Walk sideways! Sideways!"

They walked a ways and took a right onto Main Street, heading past the chamber of commerce and the memorial library. They passed a bus station and a coffee shop and a bank. Cars driving along the road slowed down to look at Elaine in her mask with the glasses on the outside and Lucida in her cat-burglar outfit.

"Maybe we ought to take these off, now that I think of it," said Lucida, straightening up from her crouch. "I think we're attracting attention."

They removed their masks and continued. Ten minutes later, they were in front of Croton's house.

"Are you sure he's not home?" asked Elaine as they huddled between two rhododendron shrubs lining the side of the house. Lucida switched on her flashlight.

"Shh. Positive. He goes to the movies and then out for burgers and shakes with his shallow theater friends. They sit around and gossip. It's disgusting."

Lucida withdrew something that looked like a pen from her back pocket. She clicked on the end and pulled out the top so it stretched like a television antenna. Elaine watched as it grew longer and longer, until it was taller than both of them.

"What is that?"

"Shh."

She took out a round mirror that looked like it came out of a compact and removed a wad of pink gum from her mouth. She spread the gum on the back of the mirror and stuck it to the end of the metal stick.

"What are you doing?"

"I saw this in a movie once." She pressed her back against the concrete foundation of the house and moved sideways, in short jerks, very slowly, behind the rhododendron bush until she was just below a window. The light was on inside.

"Are you crazy?" Elaine whispered. "Get back here!"

"Shine the flashlight," Lucida whispered back, tossing it over.

Elaine watched as Lucida slid the long handle of the pen/antenna through her hands until the end with the mirror was at the very bottom of the window. Elaine pointed the light at the mirror. She noticed she was feeling hot.

"See?" Lucida whispered from behind the rhododendron. "There they are. Just like I said. Watching television in the den."

The pink blob of Lucida's gum fell off the end of the stick, and the mirror disappeared into the shrubbery.

"Damn," said Lucida, snapping her pen together. "I wanted to show you. Oh well, they're in there. Trust me. Let's go to the front."

They bent down and ran around the back of the house, tiptoeing past a covered pool and some lounge chairs. When they got to the front door, Lucida pulled a paper clip and two bobby pins out of her front pocket. She stuck one pin between her teeth and unfolded the paper clip. Then, her tongue sticking out alongside the pin, she fiddled with the lock for a few minutes.

"What are—what are we going to do if they hear us before we get in?" Elaine whispered.

Lucida shrugged as she worked the lock. "We'll improvise. Maybe just say I was in the neighborhood and stopped by to say hello."

Elaine whispered, "We might say we were taking an informal poll for my mother, to garner votes for the upcoming congressional election."

Lucida beamed at Elaine in the light underneath the front porch.

"I'm proud of you, Elaine. You are really coming along." She pressed her lips together, jiggled the paper clip and the pin in unison, and leaned into the door. It opened with a soft click.

"Follow me," she whispered.

They squeezed through the doorway and got down on all fours. Lucida motioned for Elaine to shut the door. They could hear the sounds of the television from the back of the house, a program with a laugh track.

"Do what I do," Lucida whispered. She got down on

her stomach and half crawled, half slid across the wall-to-wall carpeting, through the front of the house and to the opening leading to the hallway. She paused at the bathroom and sat down with her back against the doorjamb. She pulled her knees up to her elbows. Elaine sat across from her and did the same.

"This is the most dangerous part," Lucida said, shining her flashlight to the end of the hallway, although it was perfectly well lit. "Croton's bedroom is the last door on the left. See there? But the door right opposite, that's the den. If someone comes out while we're in the hallway, we're sunk. There's nowhere to hide. Got it?"

Elaine nodded, thoroughly horrified. She wondered what she had been thinking to let herself get involved in an ordeal of this type. She vowed if she ever got out of Croton Harmon's house that she would never, ever, for the rest of her days allow Lucida to put her up to any more schemes. She made herself a promise and an oath.

The two girls slid down the hallway like a pair of sidewinders.

"Head down," Lucida whispered fiercely. And then, horribly, the door to the den opened. Elaine saw an ankle and a black sock in a brown slipper at the end of the hall. It stayed there a moment.

"Where'd you say they were?" A man's voice filled the hallway.

"In the red tin. Next to the coffee machine."

Lucida dove into a closet, reaching around the door and pulling Elaine in with her just as Mr. Harmon headed out of the den and down the hallway toward the kitchen.

"I don't know if we have any more," a woman's voice echoed down the hall, over the laugh track. "I think Croton ate them all."

"Damn him," Mr. Harmon grumbled, shuffling around in the kitchen.

"I thought you said there was nowhere to hide," said Elaine, unwinding the cord of the vacuum cleaner from her foot. Her heart pounded in her head.

Lucida put her fingers to her lips.

"You're missing the program!"

"There's no more damn cookies!"

"Just a minute." Another set of feet, presumably Mrs. Harmon's, stepped into the hallway. Lucida and Elaine listened to the opening and closing of cupboards and the sound of something being taken out of the freezer or the refrigerator.

"Why, you can't find anything for yourself, you're as bad as your son."

Elaine promised herself that she would never, ever again, not ever, in the interest of saving time, purchase canned chicken stock instead of making it from scratch. She swore she would begin a regimen of bread baking, even though it was much easier to buy a baguette at the market. She would improve her *bouillabaisse*. She would devote her life to keeping a skin from forming on the top of a custard, to keeping the butter chilled in the pie dough.

"Are you all right?" Lucida asked after the Harmons had gone back down the hallway to the television and the den. "You're dripping wet."

Elaine could barely summon a nod, her eyes slits, her blouse drenched.

"Okay, let's go!"

Lucida pushed open the closet door with her foot. The girls once again crawled out into the hallway. When they were sure the passageway was clear, they stood up and ran as quickly and as quietly as they could all the way to the last door on the left, which Lucida pushed open and then shut, painstakingly, with the tiniest of clicks. She switched on the light.

"Phew," Lucida said.

"Turn off the light," Elaine said. "They'll see it."

"No, they won't. They're watching their show, just like

they do every Friday night. We'll be out of here before their program ends."

Elaine took off her glasses and wiped her forehead with the back of her sleeve. "Lucida, I feel—I don't believe I can manage this type of anxiety."

But Lucida was already rummaging through Croton's desk drawers.

"I know he keeps that list somewhere in here. Do me a favor, will ya? Go through his night-table drawer. It's over there on the other side of the bed." Lucida pushed the papers and pencils around inside the desk and reached far back into the drawer, but she only came up with a box of paper clips and a stack of photographs of Croton. Elaine looked around the room, which had pictures of Croton in various poses and outfits on every wall.

"Narcissist," Lucida said, sitting down at the desk and flipping through photo after photo of Croton in the classroom, at the gym, lying by the pool.

"There's nothing in this drawer except this," said Elaine, holding up a framed five-by-seven photograph of Croton standing on the beach in a Speedo.

Lucida sighed. "So handsome."

"I want to get out of here. Now!"

"Hold on. That stupid list has got to be in one of these

drawers." Lucida jerked open a side drawer and there was a terrible crash as the bottom gave way and more photos of Croton fell onto the floor.

The girls froze in terror. A laugh track sounded loudly from the den. Lucida relaxed.

"I forgot about that drawer. Shoot. Now we're going to have to put everything back and fix it."

"Lucida," Elaine said, in a strained whisper. "I don't see any kind of list of theaters here."

Lucida looked away from Croton's old homework papers with Fs circled at the top, a few old playbills, more photos of himself on the stage.

"You're right," she said. "He must have moved it. We'll have to search."

"Let's leave now."

"I'm not leaving without that list."

Lucida jammed the broken drawer back in place and looked in the one beneath it, but there was nothing there except some stage makeup and hair wax.

"Where could he have put it?" She stuck out her bottom lip and blew up her bangs over one eye. "Oh, wait, I know."

Elaine went over to the other side of the bed and crouched down in the corner.

"What are you doing? You have to help me."

Elaine scrunched herself into a ball between the bed and the corner wall, just below a painting of Croton Harmon as Peter Pan.

"Well, just a second. I think I remember he had a secret drawer in the dresser here. . . ." Lucida went to his dresser, which had a large black-and-white head shot of Croton with his shirt unbuttoned on top of it.

"Aha!" Lucida opened the top drawer and lifted out a small box. She took out a few vials of cologne samplers, unfolded a magazine photo of a man wearing a pashmina. She took out a lipstick.

"I wonder who this is for," Lucida said, examining the lipstick.

"Maybe it's his," said Elaine from behind the bed. "Please, Lucida, I think I may be sick."

"It's got to be in here somewhere," said Lucida. She dug around some more, pulling a folded piece of paper out of a white envelope.

"Here it is!"

At that moment, unfortunately, both Lucida and Elaine heard voices and footsteps coming down the hall. Lucida turned white.

"Holy Shakespeare, it's Croton. What's he doing home so early?"

The footsteps grew closer. Lucida slammed shut the box and shoved everything back in the top drawer. She crawled across the bed to where Elaine was squashed in the corner and jumped on top of her.

"Get down, get down!"

"What the—" said Croton as he pushed open the door to his room. "Mom!" he hollered. "Have you been in my room? Why is the light on?"

"No, Croton," Mrs. Harmon called from the den.

From the other side of the bed, Lucida lay on top of Elaine, mashing her against the carpet and the wall so that she could hardly breathe.

"She's always messing around in my things," Croton remarked, just as Elaine realized there was another person in the room. Between the carpet and the edge of the bedspread, Elaine could see a polished pair of shoes walk to the closet. She heard the sound of hangers being moved around.

"My mom, too," said the other person in the room. A pair of new high-top sneakers stood behind the polished shoes.

"Oh, no," Lucida whispered. "It's someone from the idiot brigade."

"There's the one I was telling you about," Croton was saying. "From one of my first shows. The director painted that picture himself, actually."

"I always thought Peter Pan was played by a girl," said the other boy.

"The director thought I had enough feminine traits to pull off the role. I was only nine."

The bedsprings creaked as Croton sat down.

"You can sit at my desk," he said. "Don't mess anything up, though."

"I won't."

"Do you want to see the pictures from the drama club ski weekend? I had an amazing new jacket. Where were you, anyway? I don't remember seeing you there."

"I got into that accident the first day, remember?"

"Not really. Was it serious?" Croton's polished black shoes got up from the bed and moved to the closet door again.

"I guess. I was in that wheelchair for a while. And I only stopped wearing the neck brace a week—"

"Do you want to see my new head shots?"

Lucida whispered to Elaine, "I think I dropped the paper on top of the bed."

Elaine gave Lucida a terrible look.

"I've got to reach over the bed and get it," she whispered.

Elaine shook her head.

"Before he comes back from looking at himself in the mirror."

"—and Mandy and Dan and the other kids from the senior show sent those get-well cards. Don't you remember?"

"Sort of. Is my hair sticking up in the back?"

"No. It looks fine to me."

Lucida reached one arm over the bed and felt around for the folded-up piece of paper.

"Did you hear something?" the boy said suddenly. The high-tops turned and pointed in the direction of the bed.

"No," said Croton. "Do you like this shirt? It's got a ruffle at the waist."

"I thought I heard something. Like paper rustling."

"I'm not sure the jeans go with it, though. Feels a little too casual."

"I felt it with the tips of my fingers," Lucida whispered to Elaine. "But I need to stretch a little farther."

"So do you want to know something?" Croton said. "I've got an amazing secret that no one else at New Paltz High knows about." The black shoes moved back to the bed and the springs creaked as Croton sat down again. Lucida pulled her hand back just in time.

"What? Tell me."

Lucida pinched Elaine's ear.

"It's this incredible secret. Promise not to tell anybody?"

"Cross my heart."

"There's going to be a competition," Croton said. The bedsprings creaked again as Croton got off the bed and walked into the center of the room. Elaine could just see the ironed crease along the inside seam of his jeans.

"Yeah?"

"It's sponsored by WKTV in Kingston. Cable access. They've got a spot for a half-hour weekly program."

"Is it a big deal?"

"Big deal? Are you kidding? This is, like, the greatest thing that's ever happened in the valley. I'm going to win that slot with my own show. I've already got a name for it—*Croton Crows*. Isn't that a fabulous name? It'll be like a gossip column, only on TV. I'll talk about style. It's a perfect venue for me to showcase one of my talents."

Lucida snorted.

"Did you hear that?" said the boy. "It sounded like a pig."

"I'm going to start putting together the show this week. I got the leg up on it from Charlie Winters at the station. I knew it was a brilliant move of me to intern there over the summer. Nobody's going to know about the competition for another two weeks. I need an assistant, though. That's why I wanted to talk to you alone."

"Really? Wow, Croton. I'd be honored."

"I figure you could be my script supervisor," said Croton. "Help me figure out what to say."

"Sure. Who'll direct?"

"Mandy can handle that stuff."

"Nah, too flaky. You need someone resourceful, with plenty of smarts."

"Let me ask you something," said Croton. "What do you think of Lucida Sans?"

Lucida sat up abruptly. Elaine pulled her down again.

"That weird girl who comes to school dressed up like Napoleon?"

Lucida turned purple. She took a breath to protest, but Elaine clamped a hand over her mouth.

"Yeah. I mean—I know she looks ridiculous. And she's a terrible actor. But she's not bad with the camera. And she's good at working with talent and improvising and thinking on her feet—"

"I guess. Do you really want to be seen with her, though? Janie Perkins told me her two mothers served chocolate-covered mashed potatoes with sausage ice cream at her fourth-grade birthday party."

"Really?"

"Yes. Look, you want to hang out with Lucida Sans, that's your business. Don't be surprised when you find out she's the only friend you have left, though. Nobody likes her."

Croton let out his breath. "Yeah, I guess you're right. She is weird. I don't know what I'm thinking."

"Here's what I think your first show should be about . . ."

Lucida squashed Elaine harder against the wall as she reached around the bed, furiously patting the top of the pillow and the comforter.

"Stop that!" Elaine whispered. "They're going to see you."

"Who cares?" Lucida whispered back, feeling around some more until she found the white envelope. She stuffed it into the waistband of her black tights. "Now's our chance," she whispered. "They're busy at the desk taking notes."

"We follow you to the mall, see? You could interview small businesses catering to teen interests. . . ."

"Are you kidding?" Elaine whispered back furiously.

But Lucida had already crawled around the bed and was crossing in front of the dresser. She motioned for

Elaine to follow. They made quite a sight, the two of them, crawling along the rug of the bedroom while the boy in the white high-tops wrote notes at Croton's desk as Croton looked over his shoulder. Lucida and Elaine wriggled past.

"What about a hair salon? We could do a show about my hair that teaches other guys how to groom themselves."

"Most guys don't care about that stuff."

"They should. A lot of girls are into me because I take care of myself as well as they do."

"I guess. But a show all about your hair might seem a little self-serving."

"What about my clothes, then? Guys don't know how to dress themselves. . . ."

Elaine and Lucida made it out the bedroom door and raced down the hallway. They threw open the front door and ran as fast as they could down the street, panting and laughing wildly.

"I knew Croton would give it up!" Lucida cried. "He can't keep a secret to save his life!" They stopped running and slowed down to catch their breath. They turned the corner on Main Street in the direction of Lucida's house.

"I can't believe he didn't see us," Elaine said, shaking her head in disbelief. "How could he not have seen us?"

"And what a pushover! Croton knows I'm fifty times

smarter than that dumb Mandy. Have you ever seen anyone bend to peer pressure as much as Croton Harmon? What was I thinking to ever be involved with him?"

"You said he was handsome. You said he was your weakness."

"Did you hear what he was talking about?" Lucida tucked her flashlight into the belt of her tights, looking terribly excited.

"You mean that thing about KTV?"

"No, the part about the hair salon. Yes! Of course KTV! Now we have the same edge as he does," Lucida said, waving her arms in front of her as they walked. "All we have to do is invent our own program! We'll think of something fifty thousand times better than his narcissistic program, and we'll win the competition. See? It's the ultimate revenge. Oh, Elaine, this is just too exciting!" She was practically hopping along the sidewalk as they made their way.

"Does this mean we aren't going to send the letter?" asked Elaine, wondering if she had suffered the ordeal in Croton's bedroom for nothing.

"Nah, we'll send that, too. But now we're on to bigger and better things. Imagine! Our own cable-access program!"

If Elaine had been thinking clearly, if she had been of sound, rational mind, rather than traumatized by the memory of sneaking into Croton's house and hiding under his bed, she might have noticed that Lucida used the words "our own cable-access program." But shaken as she was from the experience, and relieved as she was to be out of Croton Harmon's bedroom, she did not really listen, and she did not really hear.

"Our own program," Elaine repeated numbly. "Imagine."

The two girls ran down the street, past the gas station and the convenience store and many fire hydrants, all the way back to Lucida's white house with the brown trim on Elting Street.

Dear Julia,

With all the fortitude my 13-year-old arms could muster, I gave five sharp blows on the handle, causing the omelette to jump over the side of the pan and slide into a crack between the stove and the refrigerator.

Yours sincerely,

Elaine Hamilton

9

The weather grew colder. Elaine practiced fluting mushrooms and made puff pastry. Lucida went to singing and theater auditions, ballet and modern dance tryouts, performance art readings, even mime. She went to the city to have her head shots taken.

"No one even returns my calls," Lucida said glumly. "How am I going to win the competition at WKTV if I can't get a callback anywhere else?" They were sitting in the cafeteria again. Elaine was eating Timbale de Choux de Bruxelles with a cream sauce. Lucida, dressed as Mother Teresa, was having the Dutchess Meat Pie.

"No ideas yet?" Elaine asked, spooning some sauce over the top of her *timbale*.

Lucida adjusted her habit so she could eat. "Nothing comes to mind," she said. "I get ideas all the time, but nothing, you know, spectacular."

Elaine ate another bite of her lunch and took a sip of water. A wine, perhaps a Bordeaux or a Côtes Du Rhone, would have gone well with her lunch, and she wished for a glass. But of course you couldn't bring a Côtes Du Rhone to high school.

"I was thinking we could do a vaudeville act. Something physical, like the Marx Brothers. Lots of catchy one-liners. I could be Groucho and you could be Harpo, since you don't talk much anyway."

"We? You mean you. As I said before—"

"But—"

"I don't want to be a part of this plan, Lucida."

"What about opera? Can you sing?"

"No," said Elaine. She arranged her napkin on her lap and forked up a little more of her timbale. The sauce was creamy and rich, the custard smooth.

"What about modern dance?"

Elaine shook her head.

"Oh, well," Lucida said, and she pushed the crust of

her meat pie to the corner of her plate. "You're kind of literary, in a way," she said a moment later. "Maybe we could memorize famous poems and dress up as the poets who wrote them."

Elaine raised her eyebrows.

"Well, it was just a thought," Lucida said. She looked at Elaine's spread for a moment. "What are you eating, anyway? What are those green flecks?"

"Timbale de Choux de Bruxelles," Elaine said.

"They look like chopped-up brussels sprouts."

"They are."

"Would you mind if I tried some?"

"Of course not," Elaine said.

"What's the runny stuff?"

"Sauce Mornay."

Lucida pressed her plastic fork into the vegetable mold and cut herself a small piece. She dipped it into the sauce, closed her eyes, and put it into her mouth. She chewed and swallowed. She opened her eyes in surprise.

"That's pretty good," Lucida said. "Your mother must stay up all night making lunches."

Elaine didn't say anything.

"Want to try the Dutchess Meat Pie? I think they put Spam in it."

"No, thank you."

"How come you never invite me over?" Lucida asked.

"Excuse me?"

"You come over to my house all the time. How come you never invite me to yours?"

Elaine squeezed her napkin. She chewed her food and took another sip of her water. She waited a long time to answer.

Finally she said, "I prefer your house."

"Why?"

"My family . . . they are . . ." Elaine trailed off a moment, staring at the lunch ladies serving the Dutchess Meat Pie. She looked back at Lucida.

"It's often chaotic," Elaine finished.

"So what? I think you should invite me someday."

"All right," said Elaine, loosening the grip on her napkin. "I'll invite you over. Someday."

Lucida grinned and ripped open two sugars and a package of relish.

Someone pushed open the door to the cafeteria and Croton walked in, followed by his group of friends. They were carrying a lot of equipment. One of the blond-haired boys pointed a large microphone in Croton's direction while a slight girl with red hair struggled to balance a video camera on her shoulder. Elaine noticed that another boy with white high-tops was walking around behind Croton with a pencil and clipboard. The blond-haired boy dropped the microphone, and a piece broke off and rolled under one of the cafeteria tables. Croton ran his fingers through his hair and looked at the ceiling.

"Look at that," said Lucida. "They've already started."

"Don't despair," said Elaine. "I'm sure you'll come up with an idea soon."

"Really?" Lucida asked, pouring another hill of sugar on her mashed potatoes.

"Yes. You'll come up with an extraordinary idea extremely soon."

"Extremely soon," repeated Lucida, spreading some vanilla ice cream on her Dutchess Meat Pie. "I like the sound of that."

The next night, a Friday, while Elaine was trussing a bird for Caneton à l'Orange, the doorbell rang. Mr. Hamilton, in his yoga tights and without a shirt, was on the telephone. The twins were sitting in the same chair, looking morose. Mr. Hamilton was sweating.

"Hello? Yes. I've been on hold a while now. A whole bottle of baby aspirin. That's right."

"A-s-p-i-r-i-n," Lynn spelled out, slowly. He was wearing a new pair of yoga tights and sitting at the kitchen table. "From the Greek."

Francis kicked a soccer ball around the kitchen. Chris was ironing a white skirt with pink stripes.

"Yes, I am sure of the brand," Mr. Hamilton was saying. "And, no, it hadn't been opened. How childproof could it be if a pair of six-year-olds got to it?"

Elaine finished with the duck and started slicing potatoes for homemade potato chips. Her mother loved potato chips.

From the chair at the kitchen table, the twins watched longingly as Elaine sliced the potatoes.

Francis faked a pass to Lynn.

"Cut it out!" Lynn yelled. "I'm trying to study."

"There are only three left in the bottle," said Mr. Hamilton, taking the folded dish towel from beneath Elaine's apron strings and wiping his forehead. "I have to assume they got them all."

"Elaynee, can't I cut the potatoes?"

"Nope," said Francis, bouncing the ball with his knee. "You guys are in big trouble. You're never going to slice a potato again. Ever."

Robyn began to cry. "We're sawreeeee, Daddy," he sobbed. Leslie joined in. "Yes, we're sawwwwreeee."

"Take deep breaths, in and out, through your nose," Lynn told the twins. "Like this. *Ohm. Ohm.*"

"No—no—please don't put me on hold again—" Mr. Hamilton looked at the receiver and sighed. He pressed the phone against his ear with his shoulder and felt Robyn's forehead. Then he felt Leslie's forehead.

The doorbell rang again.

"Will somebody please get that?" said Mr. Hamilton.

"They look fine to me," said Francis. "Serves them right if they get a stomachache."

"I don't know," said Mr. Hamilton, on the phone again. He tipped up Robyn's chin and squinted at him. Then he did the same to Leslie.

The doorbell rang a third time.

"Will somebody *please* get that?" Mr. Hamilton asked, covering the mouthpiece with his hand. Elaine took some pastry dough out of a bowl in the refrigerator. She wiped her hands on her apron, went to the front of the house, and opened the door. There, standing before Elaine as plain as anything, was Isadora Wilhelminetta Fischburger, otherwise known as Lucida Sans.

"Surprise!" Lucida cried. "Bet you didn't think it was going to be me."

"How—how did you know where I lived?" Elaine stammered.

"I looked up your name in the phone book. Aren't you going to invite me in?" She was standing on the front steps in a chiffon dress with rhinestones down the front. Her wig was flowing and blond, with a tiara on top. She clutched a handbag that was studded with fake sapphires.

"It's kind of—I'm kind of busy right now."

"Elaine, who is that?" Mr. Hamilton called from the kitchen.

"Hold on a second," said Elaine. She shut the door, leaving Lucida outside on the steps, and went into the kitchen.

"It's—it's just a friend," said Elaine, twisting her apron in her hands. "What does poison control advise?"

"I'm still on hold," said Mr. Hamilton, looking into Robyn's throat. "Who did you say was at the door?"

"Just—just a friend."

"Elaine doesn't have friends," Francis said, bouncing the soccer ball on his head. "Her friends are potatoes and shallots. And butter. Butter is Elaine's best friend."

"What friend, Elaine? That one with the familiar-sounding name?"

"Yes."

"Where is she?"

"Standing outside."

"It's twenty degrees out! What's the matter with you?"

"Disclosure," Lynn muttered. "D-i-s-c-l-o-s-u-r-e. From the Latin."

"Maybe it's not the best time to have company," said Elaine, wringing her hands in her apron.

"Oh, what's one more?" said Chris, waving the iron around. "That would only make about fifty people in the kitchen, right?" He ran the iron over a wrinkled pink stripe.

"Don't be ridiculous, Elaine. Let her in. Hello? Yes. I've been on hold for ten minutes now and my twin sons . . ."

Elaine went back to the front door and opened it. Lucida was still standing there, shivering in her chiffon.

"Thanks a lot." Her teeth were chattering.

"Sorry," Elaine said, opening the door a little wider. She was shocked and embarrassed to find Lucida at the door, and had great difficulty finding words. "My family," she managed. "They are—they are a bit—"

"Don't worry," said Lucida, taking off her white gloves. "What's your mother making? It smells great in here!"

Francis was standing in front of the ironing board, his soccer ball under his arm, when Elaine led Lucida into the kitchen.

"Who's she?" Francis asked, dropping his ball.

"I'm Lucida," said Lucida, holding out her hand. "Lucida Sans."

"Nice to meet you," said Francis. He watched Lucida look around the kitchen, taking in the scene. He stared at his feet.

"Exposure. E-x-p-o-s-u-r-e," Lynn said. Chris looked up from his ironing and stared at Lucida, a slow smile spreading on his face as he took note of the pink chiffon, the sequins and heels, the pink boa, the sparkling tiara.

"Nice ensemble," he said, putting down the iron and walking in a complete circle around Lucida.

"Well, they look fine to me," said Mr. Hamilton. "Surely there must be a natural alternative."

Lucida asked Elaine, "What's with the apron?"

"I—I just, my house is, as you can see—" Elaine stammered, and not knowing what to say or where to hide, she turned desperately to her potatoes.

"She's cooking, as usual," said Francis. "And if you're expecting macaroni and cheese, you can just forget about it."

"Well, if you say so," Mr. Hamilton was saying. "It's not something I like to do, but all right."

"Where *did* you get that dress?" Chris asked. "It's so 1978!"

"Seventy-three," Lucida said, looking pleased. "I got it at Winette's Costumery, on Herrington. They've got the vintage stuff for cheap."

"Francis," said Mr. Hamilton, hanging up the phone. "I want you to take your bike over to the drugstore and pick up something called ipecac."

"What's that?" Francis asked. He had not taken his eyes off Lucida.

"Never mind. Just go get it. The pharmacist will show you."

"Why do I have to?" Francis kicked his soccer ball against the refrigerator.

"Just do it," said Mr. Hamilton, wiping his forehead with the dish towel again and squinting at the twins, who had pushed two chairs by the sink and were sorting potato slices. He shook his head and turned to the new guest.

"Forgive my rudeness, Lucida Sans," he said, putting his hands on Lucida's shoulders and looking into her eyes. "We have heard nothing about you. And yet you loom so large on the horizon."

"Nice to meet you, Mr. Hamilton."

"Are you staying for dinner?"

"I'd love to, thanks."

Francis slammed the door. Elaine picked up the pastry and turned it over on a marble slab.

"Those shoes. Are they patent leather?" Chris asked.

Lucida shook her head. "Vinyl. But you'd never know, right?"

Chris sank into a kitchen chair, flabbergasted.

"Boys, how are you feeling?" asked Mr. Hamilton. "Do you feel dizzy or weak?"

"No!"

"We feel good!"

"I-p-e-c-a-c," said Lynn. "The dried root of a shrubby South American plant, *Cephaelis ipecacuanha*."

"You were right about my getting an idea for the video," said Lucida, adjusting her tiara and moving over to the counter where Elaine was working. "I got one right after homeroom today. I even made a video to show you," she said. "Do you have a VCR?"

"It's upstairs, in the den," said Elaine. She had been working the pastry for too long, and the butter was getting oily.

"I can't wait to show it to you. I think it's very original and creative," Lucida was saying.

"Yes," said Elaine with a pained expression. "But if you will forgive me, Lucida, I must tend to this pastry dough before the butter loses its chill."

"By all means," said Lucida, grinning and pulling out a chair at the kitchen table next to Lynn. "I can wait. I have all night."

"I like your boa, too," Chris told Lucida from across the table. "Come to think of it, there's absolutely nothing I don't like about your outfit."

Lucida beamed. "What's your name, anyway?"

"Chris. But I'm thinking of changing it to Tallulah. Can I try on your tiara?"

"Take the wig, too. It's a set."

Chris's eyes widened with love and admiration.

Elaine rolled out the dough. With a serrated roller from the drawer, she cut the dough into even two-and-a-half-inch squares. She removed a bowl of filling from the refrigerator and spooned a teaspoonful into the center of each square of dough. Then, quick as lightning, she folded one of the squares over on itself to form a triangle, pressed the edges together with her fingers, and made a crisscross design with the tines of a fork. She laid the puffy triangle on a sheet covered with parchment paper. Then she made another, and another. In six minutes she had made forty-five, painted the tops with a beaten egg, and poked a little hole at one corner of each. She opened the oven door and placed them on the middle rack.

"Wow," said Lucida.

"Yup," said Chris.

Mr. Hamilton slumped in a chair at the kitchen table.

"How about that," he said, nudging Lynn, who didn't look up from his spelling list. "A whole bottle of baby aspirin and they're up slicing potatoes like nothing."

Elaine poured some duck stock into a reduction of sugar and red wine vinegar. She beat in arrowroot and Madeira and stirred in a little orange peel. She stirred the mixture as it simmered, tasted the sauce, added seasoning. She flipped the pan and poured in some cognac, struck a match, and set the pan aflame. A blue streak flashed in the skillet, lighting up the kitchen.

"Wow," said Lucida.

"Yup," said Chris.

The kitchen was quiet except for the steady chopping sound of the twins slicing potatoes on the cutting board. Elaine adjusted the heat beneath the reduction in one saucepan and poured a sauce over some sliced pears. She checked the pastry in the oven and looked at her watch. She wiped her hands on the dish towel and took off her apron.

"All right," she said, turning around. She did not look directly at Lucida, but slightly above her head, a little to the left. "Let's go view your videotape."

"Not a chance," Mr. Hamilton said to the twins, who climbed off their chairs and began following Elaine and Lucida out of the kitchen. "I'm supposed to watch you for signs of irregular behavior."

Lucida trailed Elaine up the stairs to the den, pulling her fingers through her hair and puffing out her bangs. She opened her mouth to say something, thought better of it, shook her head, and bit her lower lip. She followed Elaine to the top of the stairs, but she moved slowly, almost painfully, because a new thought was taking shape in her mind, struggling inside her brain. She wrestled with this new thought as she climbed the stairs behind Elaine, trying, for the first time in her life, to find the right words.

"Stop!" Lucida cried, at the top of the stairs.

Elaine stopped.

"Before we go to the den," she said. "I'd like to—I mean—would you mind if we . . ."

"Yes?"

"I'd like to see your bedroom."

"Pardon?"

Lucida, her mind clearer now and getting clearer by the moment, repeated, "I'd like to see your room."

Elaine hesitated, lingering at the top of the stairs. "It's just a room, really." She barely whispered the words.

"You've seen mine. It's only fair."

Elaine rested one hand on the banister at the top of the stairs. She brought her other hand up to her face, removed her glasses, and looked at them. She stood there a few moments, just resting her hand on the banister, staring at her glasses.

"All right," she said. "I will show you my room."

She turned in the other direction and pointed to a door at the end of the hall, which hung slightly ajar. She replaced her glasses, moved forward, and now it was her turn to move slowly, to move painfully, because a new thought was taking shape in Elaine's mind, too, struggling inside her brain. She reached the door and pushed against it with her shoulder, as if it were heavy. She switched on a light.

Lucida walked into the middle of the room. There was a small desk to one side, an oak dresser, a queen-sized bed. A built-in bookshelf covered a wall by a large window. The wooden chest with the brass handles was at the foot of the bed. There were no rugs or carpets on the polished wood; the room was plain, spare, and would have been considered just another tasteful but unremarkable space if it weren't for one thing, for one detail, for one incredible and amazing and extraordinary point of interest.

Ceiling to floor, the walls were covered with photographs. Some were large and some were small, but they were all framed, all matted, mostly shot in black-and-white. And they were all of the same person—a tall woman, slightly stooped, with a large face and an apron.

Lucida stood in front of the first photograph by the door. The tall and slightly stooped woman was emptying a saucepan into a sink, her back to the camera while a cloud of sunlight poured in through the window, illuminating the edges of her face. The atmosphere was calm, peaceful, a quiet morning in the kitchen perhaps, warm and good-smelling and full of light.

Lucida stepped around the room, studying the other pictures of the tall, stooped woman. In one she was holding a pot tilted at the camera; in another she hovered over a counter with a knife and a cutting board covered with mushrooms. There were photos of the woman selecting a loaf of bread at a marketplace, sitting at a small table overlooking a bay of sailboats, standing behind a counter holding a gigantic fish. There was a picture of her as a younger woman, sitting in a velvet chair and holding a cat, looking directly into the face of the observer with a keen smile on her face.

"Are these all of the same—the same person?" Lucida asked, touching the face of the woman in one of the photographs. "Is this—"

"Julia Child," said Elaine. She sat on the edge of her bed and looked at the ceiling.

Lucida looked at each photograph, moving silently around the room as if she were viewing a museum exhibit. When she had finished, she went to the bookshelf by the large window and looked at some of the titles. *Mastering the Art of French Cooking, Volume One* and *Volume Two, The French Chef Cookbook, The Way to Cook, Cooking with Master Chefs*. There were other titles, too, books on French cooking techniques, on the history of French cuisine, on practical methods for preparing vegetables and poultry, on artisanal cheeses, charcuterie, soups and hors d'oeuvres, desserts. There was an entire shelf of books about pastry and on another, the art of bread baking.

Elaine sat hunched at the edge of the bed, her shoulders forward, as if she were trying to fold herself up like a piece of paper. She took off her glasses and looked down at her shoes.

"Moms used to watch her show when I was little," Lucida said, picking up another framed picture on Elaine's desk. "They said she was an all-American original. That she set a standard for everybody."

Elaine nodded.

"Too bad Moms never picked up any of her cooking skills," Lucida said. She traced the outline of the figure in the picture, tilting her head at the image of the apron, the dish towel tucked at the waist, the enormous knife. "Can I ask you something, Elaine?"

Elaine pressed her fingers to her temples, leaned over, and stared at the wooden floor.

Lucida put the photograph back down on the desk and sat next to Elaine at the edge of the bed. "Do you remember that first day we met? The day of the fire at the Festival on the Green?"

Elaine touched the edge of her bedspread.

Lucida ran her fingers through her short hair again, puffing it out between her fingers. "Remember we went to the Muddy Cup after?"

Elaine nodded. "You put twelve packets of sugar into your coffee."

"Remember I asked you if you had a dream? A secret wish?"

"Yes," Elaine said, and she whispered the word so softly that Lucida could barely hear her.

"Well, I was just wondering, Elaine, I mean, well—is this your dream? Is this the thing you wouldn't tell me that day a long time ago? That you secretly wish to be a cook?"

Elaine nodded, knowing her secret was out in the open, finally, and that there was nothing she could do about it. She drew in her breath and waited for the laughter to come, or the scorn, or at the least for Lucida to tell her that spending time around saucepans and casseroles was much too domestic a dream in nature and had little to do with furthering the cause of gender equality or deconstructing traditional family roles. She waited for Lucida to smirk and tell her that modern dance or the performance arts were more valuable and noteworthy pursuits. But the funny thing was, Lucida didn't laugh or smirk or look scornful. She didn't say any of the things that Elaine thought she would say. In fact, she didn't say anything. Oddly enough, Lucida seemed to be waiting for *Elaine* to say something.

"Yes," Elaine said at last. She straightened up and replaced her glasses. She looked directly into Lucida's eyes. "Someday I wish to be a chef."

Lucida opened her fake sapphire-encrusted handbag and took out the videotape. She held it in her hand and looked at it, as if she were feeling its weight. Then, suddenly, she slid it from the case, flipped open the plastic cover, and in one swift jerk, pulled out a length of the magnetic ribbon. She tore off a piece and threw it on the floor. Then she pulled out some more, tearing and yanking reams of ribbon and throwing the pieces at their feet.

"What are you doing?" Elaine cried in alarm.

Lucida pulled out the last bit of film, threw the videotape to the floor, and stomped on it until it cracked and shattered.

"There," she said. She was out of breath. "There." She picked up the plastic bits and piles of torn ribbon and threw the whole thing in the wastepaper basket by Elaine's desk.

"I don't understa—"

"All this time I've been trying to figure out how to get famous. I've been dancing and singing and acting and practicing." She slumped onto the bed, shaking her head in disgust. "I went to a flamenco-dancing audition last week," she said.

Elaine covered her mouth with her hands and tried not to laugh.

"And all this time," Lucida went on, "you've been quietly filleting and chopping and sautéing and flambéing—perfecting your art and working steadily toward your dream." She bit her lower lip. "You're the genuine article, Elaine," she said. "I can only bathe in your resounding splendor."

"No, Lucida. Remember the day you played Don Quixote? I thought that was—"

"The truth is, I don't know what I want to be," Lucida said, fingering the beads on her necklace. "I'm still trying to figure it out. But you don't have to wear a mouse costume to school. You don't have anything to prove to anybody." Lucida threw her handbag into the trash with the videotape. "I could just kick myself," said Lucida, kicking herself.

"Oh, don't do that," said Elaine, getting up from the bed and taking Lucida's purse out of the wastebasket. She lay it on the bed. She began to say something, but she paused, looking nervous.

"May I suggest," said Elaine, looking shy, suddenly, "may I suggest that these past three months have been the most entertaining of my life." She sat down next to Lucida.

"I'm glad I met you," she said.

Lucida and Elaine sat on the bed side by side, looking at the photographs of Julia Child.

Lucida said, "I think I have another idea."

"You do?"

"Yes. For a show. I think there is a way to fulfill both our dreams at the same time. But you've got to trust me, Elaine. Do you trust me?"

"No."

"Good." Lucida picked up her handbag again. She paced around the room. "Yes, yes," she said, thinking aloud. "This would work. I'm sure of it. This is big. It's big, Elaine. Do you hear me? I've got it. We're going to be famous, Elaine, famous! By the way, does it smell like something's burning to you?"

"The reduction," Elaine said, jumping up and tying on her apron. "I forgot about the reduction!"

Mrs. Hamilton was so happy that Elaine had a guest over for dinner that she had two servings of Caneton à l'Orange and extra homemade potato chips. The pastry turnovers were beautiful, and when Mr. Hamilton spooned up a taste of the burned reduction, he beamed and said that it was delicious, Elaine, just delicious. Lucida told Chris she would take him to Winette's Costumery, and she told Lynn that nothing would be more thrilling than to attend the regional spelling bee finals. Francis stared at Lucida all through dinner and looked at his shoes when she smiled at him. Robyn and Leslie threw up right before Elaine served the chocolate mousse. All in all, it was a nice evening, the best Elaine had had in quite a long time.

10

The next week at school, Lucida slipped Elaine a note as she passed her in the hallway. This is what it said.

Come to my house after school today. I have plans for us. Big plans!
Lucida Sans

Elaine rode the bus with Lucida back to her house on the condition that she would be home in time to pound halibut for Quenelles de Poisson that evening. After they put down their things in the bedroom, Lucida clapped her hands together and said, "I was up half the night getting everything ready. Follow me!"

Elaine jumped when she saw all the pots and pans and knives of every size strewn across the kitchen counter, the measuring cups and spoons and spatulas piled up on the stove. A musty smell permeated the kitchen.

"Forgive the crudeness of the kitchen studio," Lucida said as Elaine walked around touching the items. "I put together the makings of a working kitchen, but"—she paused to blow some dust off a spatula—"most of the equipment has been in the basement for a while."

"It's all very nice," Elaine said, looking around appreciatively. Then, noticing the camera affixed to the tripod in front of the pantry, she asked, "What is that?"

"It's a camera," Lucida said, grinning, as she pulled out a black beret and put it on. She picked up a megaphone, unfolded a green chair by the tripod, and sat down. "You know, a recording device."

"Yes, I know. I mean, of course. But what do you intend to use it for?" Elaine asked. An uncomfortable feeling tugged at her insides.

"What do you mean, what am I going to use it for?" said Lucida, scribbling something in chalk on a slate board. "You're going to do a cooking demonstration. And

I'm going to videotape it. This is your big break, get it?"

It's hard to describe the expression, or expressions, that passed across Elaine's face in the long silence that followed Lucida's words. First there was a look of confusion, then one of slow realization, then disbelief. Next came surprise; after that, shock, and then, finally, horror.

"Are you crazy?" Elaine walked out of the kitchen and into Lucida's bedroom, where she collected her schoolbag and books. She picked up her coat. Lucida put down her megaphone and followed behind.

"Stop, Elaine. Wait!"

Elaine stopped at the front door. She waited.

"If you would just listen to my idea," Lucida said.

Elaine let out a long sigh.

"Look. You say you want to be a famous chef—"

"No, Lucida," Elaine interrupted. "I said I wished to be a chef. I never said I wanted to be famous. I want only to go to Paris, to the Cordon Bleu, to master French cuisine so I can teach others how to—"

"Well, who are you going to teach, Elaine? How will you make a name for yourself as a teacher and a chef if nobody's heard of you? You think the waitresses in whatever diner you get a job in are going to care to listen to your instructions on the practice of deglazing or the finer points of slicing a mushroom? Don't you even want to own a restaurant someday?"

Elaine hesitated.

"I don't know," Elaine said, looking as though she had not considered this possibility. "I suppose I had envisioned apprenticing with someone talented. . . ."

"Nuts, Elaine. You don't want to start out a nobody. You want to make a name for yourself right out of high school so the great chefs are begging you to work in their fancy restaurants. And the way to make a name for yourself is to make a videotape showcasing your skills. Besides, with a gift like yours for cooking, you owe it to the public to share your know-how. What does your mother say? Ask not what New Paltz can do for you, ask what you can do for New Paltz. This community could use a local celebrity, believe me."

"I—I've never performed in front of a camera before," said Elaine, twisting the arm of her coat and moving away from the door a little.

"It's easy," said Lucida. "I'll teach you." She took Elaine's bag and put it in the closet.

"I'm not sure I could explain techniques to someone who wasn't—you know—who wasn't six years old. I have no experience in it, you see."

"Don't worry." Lucida took Elaine's arm and led her back into the kitchen. "You'll be terrific. You'll be amazing."

Once they were back in position, Lucida adjusted the tripod and pointed the camera at Elaine.

"Now this is just a rehearsal," she explained. She put her director's cap back on and sat down in the chair. She lifted her megaphone.

"Camera, lights, action—"

"Wait," Elaine said, looking around the kitchen in confusion. "What are we—what technique am I demonstrating?"

Lucida shrugged. "Just put something together like you did the night I stayed for dinner." She leaned back in the chair and put one hand on the camera.

"But I need ingredients, Lucida, I can't just—"

"Can't you make something up? Something not too fancy?"

Elaine looked around the kitchen. There was a long silence.

"What sort of grocery items do you have?" she asked, looking a little frightened.

Lucida got up from her director's chair and rummaged around in the refrigerator.

"Wonder Bread," she called out, after a moment. "Some bologna. Here's an orange, but it looks a little dusty. Oh, and here's a bag of apples, but I don't know how old they are—"

"How about butter? Do you have any butter?"

"We've got a lot of butter," Lucida said, opening the freezer. "Moms always buy extra for when they make their clam-and-egg-salad dish."

"We might be able to assemble a dessert," Elaine said thoughtfully, as she walked around the kitchen opening cabinet doors and looking at the contents of the shelves. "A charlotte, maybe. Do your mothers have a liquor cabinet?"

"It's in the living room."

Elaine went to the living room. She opened the cabinet and began moving bottles around.

"I don't know if we should be in there," Lucida began. "Moms—"

Elaine read the label on a large bottle. "This will work," she said. She carried the bottle into the kitchen and placed it on the counter. She found a dish towel and tucked it into her waist. Then she washed and dried her hands. Lucida went to the camera and looked through the viewfinder.

"The lighting isn't ideal, of course," Lucida said, peering into the viewfinder, "but it will have to do."

Elaine found a casserole dish that was about three and a half inches deep. She removed the Wonder Bread and the bag of apples from the refrigerator. She took out the apples and picked up a knife.

"Hold on a second. I'm not ready. Okay. I think I'm ready. No, wait. Okay, now. And . . . lights, camera, action!" Lucida snapped the clapper board and sat down in the director's chair.

Elaine washed the apples and transferred them to the cutting board. She peeled, quartered, and sliced the first apple, and then she did another. Then another. She had made her way through ten apples when Lucida turned off the camera.

"Cut!"

Elaine looked up, startled.

"Your technique is great," Lucida said, pushing back her director's cap and blowing up air beneath her bangs. "But you've been slicing for four minutes and you haven't said anything."

Elaine blinked.

"You aren't speaking," Lucida repeated.

"But there's no one to talk to," said Elaine.

"You have to pretend there's someone there."

"Oh, well. Oh. All right. Okay."

Lucida pushed the record button. Elaine picked up her knife.

"Youmustplacetheapplesinapan—"

"Too fast!"

"You . . . must . . . place . . . the . . . apples . . . in . . . a . . ."

"Too slow!"

"In a pan," Elaine began again, wiping the back of her forehead with the hand wielding the knife, "and cook them over a very low heat for about twenty minutes, stirring occasionally, until tender."

Elaine looked up at the camera in terror, as if it were a monster about to devour her.

"Cut!"

Lucida switched the camera off again and stood up. She studied Elaine for what felt like a very long time.

"Elaine," she said, rubbing the back of her neck. "I don't mean to criticize."

"Of course not," said Elaine.

"I don't want to *judge* you or anything."

"Naturally," Elaine answered.

"Can I ask you—have you never—really never—worked in front of a camera before?"

Standing in front of her mountain of apple slices, Elaine thought hard.

"Maybe when I was young," she said. "But so many of these childhood performances are impromptu—"

"In other words, no, you have never worked in front of a camera."

Elaine shook her head. "Not really," she said.

"Let me give you a small tip. Not to criticize or judge. Just, to be, you know, as your friend, helpful."

"Naturally," said Elaine helplessly.

"May I suggest that you look into the camera every so often? Every few seconds, say?"

"Well, I—"

"I assure you it would make a difference."

"I have to pay attention to my knife."

"Imagine," Lucida said, sitting back down in her director's chair, "that the camera is another person in the room. A person you are explaining the precise instructions for making an Apple Charley."

"As if I were speaking to the twins, you mean? Even though they're not really there?"

"Yes, exactly."

"All right," said Elaine. She smoothed her apron and picked up the knife. "All right."

"Ready?"

Elaine looked into the camera. She narrowed her eyes

a little, looking a bit stern. She took a deep breath.

"While your apples are simmering, take out twelve slices of bread and remove the crusts. Cut a square and four semicircles to fit the bottom of a mold."

Lucida looked in the viewfinder and gave Elaine the thumbs-up sign.

Elaine quoted, "'Any kind of a cylindrical mold or dish will do for the operation, but the dessert will be more spectacular if your mold is the charlotte type, three and a half to four inches deep, like that illustrated in the *soufflé* section on page 162.'"

Lucida looked confused.

Elaine put down her knife and removed her apron. She laid it on the countertop. "I can't do this, Lucida," she said. "It's too difficult."

"No, it's not. Just now you were getting the hang of it."

"I feel anxious and out of sorts."

"That's natural. Don't worry."

"I feel I'm not meant for the stage."

"Look," said Lucida. "Stand by the camera and watch me. I'll model the technique."

Lucida put on an apron. She picked up the knife and smiled into the camera for a very long time. Then she chopped a slice of bread into ten pieces, all the while gazing into the camera and tossing her hair so abruptly that her beret fell off. Then, as part of a tap dance, she half sang, half spoke the words: "An Apple Charlene is one of the finest examples of French Cuisinart known to man. Since the dawn of the gorilla, prehistoric man has eaten Bavarian crèmes while flambéing the famous Molotov Cocktails." She pirouetted around the island counter, picked up the knife, and whacked at another slice of bread. She beamed and winked at the camera lens. She held a piece of bread underneath her chin as a final pose.

Elaine sighed. "You possess such natural gifts," she said. "Only a true master of the stage could achieve such subtlety."

"Well, I wasn't born with my gifts," said Lucida, still beaming. "I had to practice."

"Lucida, I don't think I can complete my performance."

"Oh, come on. Why don't you just finish up and I'll tape through without any more interruptions. We can analyze the whole thing later."

Elaine nodded and picked up the knife one last time. Lucida turned on the camera. Elaine trimmed bread slices to fit the mold and explained that clarified butter was the separation of liquid and milk particles over moderate heat.

Lucida went to the corner store twice—once for vanilla extract and whipping cream, another time to buy preserves. Elaine filled the mold with apple purée and placed it on the middle rack of a preheated 425-degree oven.

"Well, I'm glad that's over," said Lucida, removing the fourth videotape from the camera as Elaine finished with the dishes. "You know, I think you're getting the hang of it."

"Really?" Elaine asked, putting down her dish towel and walking toward the hall closet to get her things.

"Yes," said Lucida. "Looking into the camera every twenty minutes may not be ideal, but, well, it's a starting point anyhow."

"I appreciate the encouragement," said Elaine, with a breath of relief.

"Shall we review the tape tomorrow afternoon?" Lucida asked, following Elaine to the front door. She opened it, and a rush of cold air came into the hall.

"All right," said Elaine. "But tomorrow I promised the twins I would let them help me make a *croquembouche*."

"I'll come to your house," Lucida interrupted. "We can review it when you're done."

"All right," said Elaine.

"Don't forget to practice," Lucida said. "Pretend the twins are a camera. Pretend everything is a camera!"

11

Lucida reviewed Elaine's performance and decided lack of practice was the only obstacle to beating Croton Harmon and winning their own show. Hour after hour, day after day, Elaine roasted chickens, assembled salads, puréed soups, and blanched vegetables in front of the camera. She made some of the most delicious and best-looking meals of her life. Mrs. Fischburger Number One and Mrs. Fischburger Number Two ate and ate, and were amazed, but in the end Lucida always put down her megaphone and shook her head.

"Too stiff," she would say, as Elaine served venison cutlets with *purée de marrons* and roasted *alouettes*. "Smile into the lens. Don't look away from the camera!"

"Use simpler language," she would say, poking a furry microphone into a sauté pan of cooking *lardons*. "And stop gasping." (Elaine tended to wheeze when she got nervous.)

But try as Lucida did (and she tried very hard), no amount of prodding or pushing or encouraging helped Elaine to relax.

"Please remember," Elaine said, after a two-hour silence during which she prepared potted shrimps on toast with Alsatian wine, Sole Bonne Femme, and *loup de mer*. "I was not trained for the stage." She wiped her brow with the dishcloth tucked in at her waist and shrugged her shoulders helplessly. "I still think you should find some other way to win your cable-access program."

But Lucida was determined.

"You have too much culinary talent," she said, shaking her head. "As your director and producer I cannot give up on you yet."

One evening, during an especially fine meal of Gnocchi à la Florentine, Mrs. Fischburger Number One took a sip of wine and said, "I hate to bring this up, as the food has been so wonderful, but why don't you try taping in your own kitchen? You might feel more comfortable."

"You mean my home?" Elaine asked, pouring some wine into Mrs. Fischburger Number Two's glass. "Oh, no. With all due respect, Mrs. Fischburger—"

"Please, Elaine, call me Sue."

"With all due respect, Mrs. Fisch—Mrs.—Sue. My—my brothers would only get in the way. Francis would throw a football, and Chris would break a nail, and Lynn would spell everything. Or the twins would cry and my father would sweat into the *demi-glace*."

Mrs. Fischburger Number One laughed a little. She helped herself to a fourth serving of Gnocchi à la Florentine and pointed to where Lucida was sorting through an alarming pile of videotapes in the living room next to the television. "Why not show them one of your programs? You might be surprised by their insight."

"Yes, you might be," said Mrs. Fischburger Number Two.

"After all, they have been watching you cook for years," said Mrs. Fischburger Number One.

"Many years," added Mrs. Fischburger Number Two.

"Oh, I don't think so," said Elaine. "I don't think they'd have any ideas."

"You never know—" said Mrs. Fischburger Number One.

"—until you try," finished Mrs. Fischburger Number Two.

"I hate to be the one to admit that the Moms are right," Lucida said later, when they were back in her bedroom with the candy-striped rug. "But it might be worth a shot. They're your family, after all. At this point I'll try anything."

"Please don't try anything," Elaine said.

But Lucida's mind was made up.

"What you are about to witness," Lucida began, standing in front of the television set in the den as she addressed Elaine's brothers, "is the culmination of weeks of collaboration between Elaine Hamilton, resident master chef and teacher extraordinaire, and myself, the producer and director of WKTV's soon-to-be-award-winning television program on cable access—"

"We get it," said Chris, who was sitting beside the twins in Mrs. Hamilton's pink bathrobe and curlers. "Put in the tape."

"Where's Francis?" asked Lucida, looking around.

"Never mind him," said Chris. "He has no appreciation for art."

"Yeah," said Lynn. "He has no appreciation."

Lucida pushed the tape into the machine and pressed the play button, and her voice cut across the dark screen.

"Lights, camera, action!" she said. A shadowy figure crossed in front of the camera, switched on an overhead lamp, and crossed back the other way.

"Is that Lucida?" asked one of the twins.

"Yes, *shh*," said Chris.

In the center of the frame, in the center of a kitchen, stood Elaine, a white apron tied firmly around her midriff, a dish towel tucked into her apron. She was gripping a knife. Her hand was shaking.

"Um, hello," she said, beginning to sweat. She wiped her face with a paper towel. "Welcome to—to my show. Today we are going to make a dish called Filets de Poisson Gratinés à la Parisienne. It's a—it's a dish fish. I—I mean, a fish dish."

"Uh-oh," Chris whispered to Lynn.

"What's going on in here?" Francis asked, spinning his basketball on his fingertips as he came into the den.

"Elaine's going to be a cooking star," Lynn said.

"No kidding?" He separated the twins and sat down between them.

"Ouch!" cried Robyn.

"Hi, Francis," said Lucida.

"Oh, um, hi, Lucida," said Francis.

"Be quiet," Chris said. "I can't hear the TV."

"But she's not saying anything," Lynn said. "She's just chopping up a fish."

"Uh-oh," said Chris.

"It involves only a few steps," Elaine was saying on the videotape, after a long and uncomfortable silence during which she carefully separated the fillet. She leaned over the countertop. Only the top of her head was visible. "You just have to follow the basic, um, basic recipe for Filets de Poisson Pôchés au Vin Blanc, and then add the new sauce, which has egg yolks and—and other things."

There was another long pause.

"Oh, boy," Chris repeated.

"*Shh*," said Lucida. "It gets better." She bit her lip. "I think."

Everyone sat in the den together, Francis on the sofa in between the twins with his basketball, Chris in his pink bathrobe and curlers, Lynn with a large tub of popcorn and his too-tight tights. The twins sucked their thumbs as they stared at the screen, watching Elaine prepare an entire meal, speaking only when Lucida called out to her, answering questions and explaining steps only when Lucida prodded or pushed, encouraged, pleaded, even begged. They sat there, all together and in the dark, watching Elaine until she could no longer bear to watch herself. She stood up and walked out of the room.

"Hey!" Lucida cried, switching off the television. "Where are you going?"

Robyn, who had fallen asleep on Lynn, woke up and took his thumb out of his mouth. Lucida ejected the videotape and ran after Elaine down the stairs to the kitchen. Francis followed Lucida, Chris followed Francis, Lynn followed Chris, and the twins ran behind.

"What's the matter?" Lucida cried. "You were just starting to hit your stride."

"After an hour and a half? We're only supposed to submit a twenty-minute videotape, Lucida."

"Well, obviously I have some editing work to do, but—"

"I can't suffer these humiliations. I recuse myself from the competition," Elaine said, opening the refrigerator.

"No, Elaynee," cried Leslie. "We want to see you on TV!"

"Come on, Elaine," said Lynn. "Don't quit. That was cool what you said—all those French words and stuff."

"Can I say something?" said Chris.

"Yeah, Elaine," Francis said as Elaine took out a carton of eggs. Using both hands, she cracked two at a time into a large bowl. "At least finish what you've started. That's what Mom always says."

Elaine turned and looked at her small audience sitting at the kitchen table. She shook her head. "I was not meant to work in front of a camera," she said, cracking the rest of the eggs. "I wish you would stop asking me to do something that's not in my nature." She attached the bowl to the electric mixer and turned it on.

"Well, fine!" shouted Lucida over the sound of the mixer, gathering together an armful of videotapes on the kitchen table and stuffing them into a black bag. "I give up. I can't force a subject to do something she doesn't want to do."

"Can I say something?" interrupted Chris, still at the kitchen table in his bathrobe and curlers.

"You work and work," Lucida went on, loudly. "You try hard to cultivate a personality. To produce a genius. But Genius must have a hand in the production of itself. If Genius wishes to hide behind a pot rack, then there's nothing I can do about it. I quit, too. I guess I'll just have to find happiness throwing batons at the mayor of New Paltz for the rest of my life." She picked up her furry microphone and hoisted it over her shoulder.

"But I think I have an idea," insisted Chris.

"Let the rotten fig win his stupid cable-access program," Lucida continued, knocking over Elaine's bowl of raw eggs with her camera bag as she swung it over her other shoulder. "Let the flower gone to seed rise to the top with his own variety show. Mediocrity pervades the media anyway. Why should any of us aspire to be anything beyond what is expected of us?"

"Can I *please* say something?" Chris interjected.

Lucida leaned against the refrigerator with her bag and microphone.

"Yeah?"

"Why don't you get in front of the camera with Elaine?" he asked.

Lucida shook her head. "That's no good," she said. "I'm the producer."

"But aren't you always involved with the theater at school—you know, singing and dancing and acting and stuff?" Chris asked.

"This is Elaine's venue," Lucida replied. "My purpose is to stay behind the scenes. As her director."

"Not that you aren't a good director," Chris said. "But I think the show would be better if you were in it." He stood up and tightened the belt on his bathrobe. He removed a pink hair curler and put it in his pocket.

Elaine turned off the electric mixer and unrolled some paper towels.

"Listen," Chris said, looking excited. "You know how on the tape you're always shouting from behind the camera—"

"I was going to take care of that in editing," said Lucida.

"And remember when you interrupted Elaine on the tape, asking what a rool was—"

"*Roux*," corrected Elaine, wiping up the raw egg from the kitchen floor.

"Yes, a roo, whatever," said Chris hurriedly. "Well, when you asked her to explain those things, she just answered you calmly, like you had just asked her what time it was and she answered, 'Oh, it's two o'clock.' You know, all casual. I think there was a moment that I could see Elaine just being herself, the way she is at home when she's teaching the twins how to dice an onion."

"Yes, but not on camera," said Lucida. "She's got to do that on camera."

"She *was* doing that on camera. But only when you were a part of the show. Know what I mean?"

"I think so," said Lucida. She put down her camera bag. "But—"

"Maybe if you get up there with her and ask her questions—you know, as if you really were a student. Like a teacher and student right in front of a television audience."

"Yeah, Lucida," said Francis, grinning shyly. "That's not a bad idea. Elaine did look calmer when you were asking her stuff."

"I want to see Elaynee on TV," Leslie cried, standing on a chair.

"Me, too," said Robyn.

"Well, I'd have to fix my hair," said Lucida, not yet convinced. "I am of course not prepared. I would need to find my character's internal motivation."

"I'll fix your hair," said Chris. "And you don't need any motivation. You could just be yourself—you know—Lucida Sans." He grinned. "I've got a whole bunch of outfits upstairs in my closet," he added.

"Choose your material," said Francis. "Chiffon, taffeta, silk-satin, lace."

"Really?" asked Lucida. "You've got silk-satin up there?"

Chris nodded, his eyes shining. "Polyester, too," he said.

"Can I help?" asked Lynn. "I want to help."

"Sure you can help," said Chris. "We'll need someone to write up dummy cards. We'll need a good speller for that."

"What about us?" Robyn cried.

"We want to help," said Leslie.

"You two are indispensable," said Lucida. She looked at Chris. "Right?"

Chris winked. "Naturally," he said. "We'll need you two to chop carrots and slice onions and measure sugar and flour and things like that. We're going to need a lot of food ready in advance, like on the real cooking shows. What do they call the people who do that stuff?"

"Sous chefs," said Elaine.

"You could teach me how to work the camera," said Francis. "You know, to handle direction and lighting."

Lucida absolutely beamed.

"And I have some ideas for the set, too," Chris went on. "We'll hang some of Elaine's pots and pans on those pegs over there, maybe put up some checkered curtains. A splash of color here, some nice tableware. Maybe a centerpiece. I have lots of decorating ideas."

Lucida said, "What do you say, Elaine? Want to go for it?"

Elaine finished wiping up the eggs. She straightened up and looked into the face of Lucida and the faces of her brothers. They stood together, waiting patiently, with earnest and hopeful looks. Chris nudged Elaine with his mother's furry slipper.

"Come on, Elaine," he said.

"Oh, all *right*," she said.

Lucida whooped and hugged Elaine. Francis took Lucida's heavy camera bag from her shoulder. Lynn went for some markers and flash cards. The twins pulled out the cutting board and Chris went upstairs to get his sewing machine. Things were about to change. You could feel it in the air.

12

They worked long hours. Chris redecorated the kitchen, arranged place settings, and sewed new curtains. Francis affixed a large mirror to the ceiling and focused the camera upward, creating the effect of looking down into Elaine's bubbling pots and steaming sauté pans on the television screen.

Lynn wrote stage directions on dummy cards that read GROUND PEPPER LEFT OF SINK or CRÈME FRAICHE BY CUTTING BOARD so Elaine could find things quickly, and Robyn and Leslie were of course useful not only as sous chefs but as two extra pairs of hands in general. Elaine and Lucida planned the menu and order of operations and decided their debut show would be something relatively simple and delicious, but classically French as well: Caneton à l'Orange.

"The problem is," Francis said, after their third day of duck roasting, "editing is a long process. How much time do we have before the deadline?"

"Five days," said Lucida as Chris pinned the hemline of her dress. "Only five days left."

"I think we're better off practicing all week and taping it live all the way through," said Francis. "We don't have time or money to deal with cutting. We'll rehearse the rest of the week and shoot on Friday. If we mess up, then we're just going to have to start all over."

"Live?" Elaine asked.

"Live on tape," said Chris, with a pin between his teeth. "Stop moving around, Lucida, or the sash will come out crooked."

"I'm tired of duck, Elaynee," said Robyn.

"Me, too," said Leslie.

Lucida nodded. "Life is hard in the entertainment world," she told them. "We'll all just have to get used to the sacrifices."

The next day, during a production meeting in the living room, Lucida brought up the idea of inviting viewers to the final taping.

"After all," she told Elaine. "There is nothing like the energy one derives from a live audience."

"Oh, no," said Elaine. "That would make me too nervous. I'll feel much better gathering people around the television for commentary and analysis."

"That sounds fine to me," said Chris, looking around. "Is anyone against the idea of just watching the final product at the end?"

Mr. Hamilton, who was passing by at this moment, overheard the last few moments of the discussion.

"Not to interrupt," he said. "But your mother will be back from the capital on Friday evening."

"Yes," Elaine murmured. "By six."

"I think she would enjoy seeing what you kids have been up to," said Mr. Hamilton. "Goodness knows I have."

Everyone looked at Elaine.

"She does enjoy the homemade potato chips that traditionally accompany Caneton à l'Orange," Elaine said, her voice nearly a whisper. She looked down at the carpet.

"Moms would probably like to come, too," said Lucida.

"So it's settled," Chris said, closing the script book. "All mothers and one father will be invited to the taping. But nobody else, in case of accidents or disasters."

"Do you think the wig is too much of a distraction?" Lucida asked Chris as the meeting broke up and they headed back into the kitchen to rehearse the end of the show once more before going home.

"Maybe if it were more of a natural color," Chris replied, adjusting a place setting in the kitchen. "Neon green is so harsh under those fluorescent lights."

"You could be right," said Lucida. "I appreciate the insight."

That Friday night Mr. and Mrs. Hamilton and Mrs. Fischburger Number One and Mrs. Fischburger Number Two sat at the kitchen table, napkins in their laps, and waited to learn how their dinner would be prepared.

"Action!" Lynn cried, snapping the clapper board. Chris cued the opening bars of a wordless tune on a tape recorder and faded the volume out as Francis adjusted the light and moved the camera closer to the counter.

"Welcome to the debut episode of *High School Chef*!" cried Lucida, holding up a steel blade and pretending to chop wildly in the air while dancing at the same time. She tossed her boa over her shoulder with great enthusiasm, and a few zebra-striped feathers floated in the air before settling into a small bowl of duck stock.

Chris snapped his fingers and Lynn held up a dummy card that read LESS IS MORE. Lucida looked surprised and hurt. She patted her wig, cleared her throat, and continued. "Today we are going to watch Chef Hamilton prepare a wonderful dish—one of the most well known of all French dishes—caneeto—canee—how do you say it, Elaine?"

"It's called Caneton à l'Orange. "

"Which means?"

"It means," Elaine said, taking a deep breath and staring into the eye of the camera, "roast duck with orange sauce."

Lynn held up a dummy card that read STOP GASPING.

"And—and I have an already-prepared roast duck here so you can see what we are—how the end product turns out."

Elaine reached behind the counter where Robyn and Leslie were hiding below the cutlery drawers. Leslie handed Elaine a plate, and Robyn dropped the duck onto it out of the line of the camera's vision.

"Isn't that beautiful," Lucida said, taking the platter and holding the duck, glistening and orange-bronzed, over her head. She was about to do a pirouette when she saw Lynn, standing behind Chris, reach for another card. She put the duck back on the counter.

"Yes," said Elaine. "It is crispy and delicious and the sauce is splendid." She glanced up at Mrs. Hamilton, who was smoothing out the wrinkles in her skirt. "But there are a few things you should know before you buy your—your duckling."

"Like what?" asked Lucida.

"Well," said Elaine. "You should only roast a duck that is six months or younger, otherwise the flesh will be tough. You can find a good four- to five-pound duckling in the frozen section of your supermarket."

"Which brings a question to mind," Lucida said. "Once, to impress my mothers, I bought a frozen chicken at the supermarket and put it in the oven right away. We had to order out that night, I recall, if memory serves."

"Well, of course you must first *defrost* the bird," Elaine said, fiddling with the napkin tucked into her waist.

Lynn held up a sign that said STOP FIDDLING.

"Probably I should have removed the plastic wrap as well," said Lucida.

STOP IMPROVISING, wrote Lynn.

"You can thaw your frozen duck in the refrigerator overnight, or just put it in running water in a pan in the sink," Elaine said, reaching down below the counter once more. Lynn handed Robyn a raw duck, which Robyn handed to Leslie, which Leslie tried to hold up for Elaine, but it slipped out of his hands and fell to the floor with a soft clomp. Leslie's eyes widened and filled with tears. Elaine panicked.

DON'T PANIC, wrote Lynn.

Lucida picked up the duck and washed it off carefully in the sink.

"As Julia once said," Lucida sang, turning off the faucet and presenting the bird,"'If you are alone in the kitchen, whoooooo is going to see?'"

Francis and Chris looked at each other and grinned.

"Pull all the loose fat from the cavity and from around the neck," Elaine said, working swiftly. "Cut out the wishbone to make carving easier, chop off the lower part of the wing, and toss it in the stockpot."

Lucida tossed the chopped parts into the stockpot.

"Remove the fat glands on the back at the base of the tail—right here—and also dig out any yellow residue that might remain. Then rub the bird all over with salt and lemon juice."

"May I try?" Lucida asked.

"Of course," Elaine replied. Robyn held up a lemon, and the salt magically appeared on the counter.

Mr. Hamilton covered a smile with his hand. Mrs. Hamilton tilted her head slightly. The Fischburger mothers nodded approvingly.

"Now, I'm just going to poke the skin at half-inch intervals," said Elaine, "along the thighs, back, and breast."

"Hasn't the duck been through enough?" said Lucida. "Now you must poke and prod it as well?"

"Yes," said Elaine, expertly pricking the skin with a fork. "This helps the subcutaneous layer of duck fat to escape during cooking. At this point you will stuff your duck with the julienne strips of simmered orange peel, which I will demonstrate in a moment. "

"How long must the orange peel strips simmer?"

"About fifteen minutes. Then you season the interior with a half a teaspoon of salt and a pinch of pepper. The last step is to truss the bird so as to make a neater presentation at table."

Elaine looked around for her trussing needle and string.

LESLIE HAS IT SOMEWHERE, wrote Lynn.

"While you search for your needle," said Lucida, leaning over the counter and flipping her red wig, "I'd like to tell a little story from my childhood that always reminds me of roasted duck. I was six years old, sitting in the bath with my rubber duckling, and—"

Chris snapped his fingers. Robyn pinched Lucida from behind the counter.

"Ow! Ow, ahem, I mean, ow—*how* do you truss a

bird anyway?" Lucida asked, but by the time Lucida had finished asking the question, Elaine had already received the needle from Leslie and was trussing the bird between thighs and wings and breast, explaining each step as she went. In one swift motion, she sewed the cavity closed.

"There," she said, patting the bird affectionately on the behind. "Isn't that lovely? Now we're all ready for roasting."

"How did you do that so fast?" Lucida asked. The truth was, Elaine worked easily with Lucida there to improvise, to ask questions, to pick up something when it fell, or to retrieve an item from the cupboard or from Lynn or Leslie or Robyn's outstretched hand. Lucida may not have been a talented chef (or a talented anything), but she was clever, thought quickly on her feet, and could ad lib her way through any mishap. And if Elaine became nervous, Lynn was always there to hold up a dummy card to remind her not to panic or pant or gasp, and when she forgot to look at the camera, she received a nudge from Lucida or Robyn. But as the minutes of the program ticked away, she made fewer and fewer mistakes, and even, at some moments, looked as though she were beginning to enjoy herself.

Elaine taught her listeners how to roast the duck and explained that the oven had to be set at 425 degrees for the first fifteen minutes and then 350 degrees for the remaining hour. She explained that basting was not necessary for a duckling since there was so much fat in the juices already, and she talked briefly about how to tell when a bird is finished roasting. Then she moved onto the orange sauce, demonstrated the process of boiling sugar with vinegar, and taught her studio audience how to make a wine reduction. She grew more and more confident as she and Lucida talked about the best way to make a good duck stock and what to use if you do not have Madeira, and Chris, watching from behind the camera, relaxed and sat back in his seat for the first time in fifteen minutes. This was it, he must have been thinking. They had a show.

Elaine placed a line of orange segments over the length of the duckling and heaped the rest at the two ends of the hot platter. She brought the platter to the table and placed it between a bowl of homemade potato chips and a bottle of chilled Corton-Charlemagne. Beside the wine was another plate of braised string beans and orange-scented carrots.

"And there you have it," said Elaine, ripping off a few paper towels from the countertop and wiping her brow.

STOP MOPPING, wrote Lynn.

"Caneton à l'Orange," Lucida repeated, putting her hands on her hips in front of the table. "What an amazing sight, Elaine. I can't wait to try your homemade potato chips."

"Yes," said Elaine, stealing a quick glance at her mother. "The reason you want to serve roasted orange duck with shoestring potatoes or potato chips is because the essence of your sauce, the scent of the oranges—this is a powerful flavor. You wouldn't want a pungent vegetable to interfere with the taste."

"Myself I am a big fan of the Dorito chip," noted Lucida. "Shall we open the Corton-Charleemag-nee?"

"Being teenagers," Elaine said, taking the corkscrew from Lucida and placing it on the table beside the wine bottle, "we cannot endorse the drinking of alcoholic beverages, but if you were of age and wished to drink an alcoholic beverage with this meal, you would want a good red Bordeaux-Médoc or a chilled white burgundy, like this Corton-Charlemagne." She hesitated, looked down, looked up, paused, and then looked up one more time and smiled, a little self-consciously, into the lens.

Francis grinned into the viewfinder of the videotape recorder.

Chris smiled from his chair at the table.

Leslie and Robyn and Lynn smiled from behind the counter.

"Thank you for sharing this meal with us," Lucida said, holding up an empty wine glass. "I'm Lucida Sans."

"And I'm Elaine Hamilton."

"And this is *High School Chef*," said Lucida.

"*Bon appétit!*"

Francis pressed the stop button on the camera and turned off an overhead light. Leslie and Lynn and Robyn crawled out from behind the counter. Elaine removed her apron. Lucida removed her wig.

"We did it, Elayneee!" cried the twins.

"You certainly did," said Mr. Hamilton, jumping up from his place in the audience and hugging the boys. He hugged and kissed the twins, and then he hugged and kissed Francis, and Francis hugged Elaine, and Chris hugged Francis. Lucida jumped up and down and shook hands with everyone and danced with the twins. Mrs. Hamilton stood up and kissed the twins as well, and congratulated Francis, Chris, and Lynn. Mrs. Fischburger Number One and Mrs. Fischburger Number Two shook hands with everyone and hugged Lucida.

"Bravo," said Mrs. Fischburger Number One.

"Encore!" said Mrs. Fischburger Number Two.

"Look at this roast duck, Elizabeth," said Mr.

Hamilton. "It's going to be delicious. Just *delicious*, Elaine."

Elaine glanced at her mother.

Mrs. Hamilton nodded at Elaine.

"We've got to review the tape, make sure it looks all right for bringing over to the station tomorrow," Elaine said.

"We're going to be a smash!" Lucida cried. "We were spectacular. We made a roast duck in twenty minutes!"

"Well, you made five roasted ducks," said Mrs. Hamilton, looking around at the frozen duck, the defrosted duck, the one that was trussed, another cooking in the oven, and the finished product at the table. "I can imagine the expense." She smiled grimly at Elaine.

"Such a talented daughter you have," said Mrs. Fischburger Number One to Mrs. Hamilton. "You must be so proud."

"Yes, well," said Mrs. Hamilton vaguely. She put a hand on her daughter's shoulder. "Maybe someday she'll write a cookbook in her spare time."

"I don't want to write," Elaine said, looking at her shoes. "I want to cook."

But Elaine had spoken too softly for anyone to hear. Mrs. Hamilton returned to her briefcase and began shuffling through papers. Mr. Hamilton started carving the bird.

"I have some work to do in my office," Mrs. Hamilton said. She straightened up. "I'll be down in a little while."

"Do you want a few potato chips to take with you upstairs?" Elaine asked.

"No, thank you, Elaine. Not tonight."

Robyn and Lynn were still jumping around behind the counter. Francis and Chris were discussing technical aspects of production and lighting problems. Mr. Hamilton uncorked the wine and poured three glasses.

"Delicious, Elaine," he said, lifting his glass. "Just delicious."

Mrs. Hamilton left the kitchen. Mr. Hamilton kept carving the Caneton à l'Orange while Chris and Francis wrote notes on a clipboard. The twins chattered with Lynn. Nobody noticed the look on Elaine's face when her mother walked out of the kitchen. Except Mrs. Fischburger Number One and Mrs. Fischburger Number Two. And Lucida. They noticed.

Mr. Croton Harmon
666 13th Street
New Paltz, NY 12561

Dear Mr. Harmon,

We are writing to inform you that we have read your new play and found yours to be quite a fresh and original new voice. We would like to find the appropriate sponsors to produce your play.

Unfortunately, timely as your story is, we are not yet convinced your story will translate to the stage. In the interest of our theater, we request that you perform a segment of the script in full costume for undisclosed viewers at the Muddy Cup, 58 Main Street, New Paltz, on Tuesday, the 22nd of October, at 2:45 P.M.

Sincerely,
Mr. I.M. Pecularis, CEO
Theater of the Obscure
New York, NY 10019

13

"What's the matter with your mother, anyway?" Lucida asked Elaine. She was lying on Elaine's bed later that evening, flipping through the pages of *Mastering the Art of French Cooking, Volume Two*.

"What do you mean?" Elaine asked, from the desk.

"You know perfectly well what I mean, Elaine Hamilton," said Lucida, snapping the book shut. "She hardly looked at you when we finished our show. She must have known we have a shot at winning that competition. We were incredible. Even Francis was jumping up and down."

Elaine stared at the top of her desk, her back to Lucida.

"She's a feminist," she said quietly.

"What's that supposed to mean?" demanded Lucida. "My Moms are huge feminists and they still think everything I do is great. Heck, *I'm* a feminist. Although," she added, after some thought, "sometimes I forget about feminism when Croton comes around."

"You don't understand," Elaine said, turning around to face Lucida. "My wanting to be a chef doesn't fit in with her plan for me. My mother was an active figure in the women's liberation movement in the seventies."

"Ring a ding ding. So were Moms."

"Julia Child learned to cook so she could prepare meals for her husband."

"So?"

"So that's not good enough for my mother. Even now, sixteen years later,"—Elaine sighed—"my mother is still trying to ratify the Equal Rights Amendment. It's her lifelong pursuit, her signature ambition—to pass that amendment. It's very controversial."

"Why?"

"Because people believe the amendment is . . . is . . ." Elaine searched for the right word. "Is obsolete."

"What's that mean?" asked Lucida.

"That it's passé. That we don't need to worry about

equal rights for women anymore. My mother doesn't believe that. She thinks we still have a long way to go until liberation. And part of that belief system involves my not taking a job that keeps me in the kitchen with stews and saucepans."

Elaine stood up and stared at the picture of Julia Child in front of the cutting board full of mushrooms.

"Being in the kitchen is symbolic for my mother," Elaine said. "It goes against everything she has worked for her whole life."

"But wait a minute," said Lucida, grabbing one of Elaine's scrapbooks from her bookshelf beside the bed and flipping through the clippings. "Doesn't it say somewhere in here that Julia Child only *started* cooking gourmet food for her husband? I could have sworn I saw something . . ." She flipped through the pages until she came to the right place.

"Look here," she said, pointing to the text and read ing. "'Julia Child, beloved cook and author, started out with little more than a humble desire to prepare French meals for her husband, Paul Child. Now, an international celebrity with over a half a million books in print, she is a household name, an educator and an icon, an influence on thousands of aspiring chefs the world over.'"

Lucida slammed the book shut and sat up.

"If that isn't entrepreneurial independence, then I don't know what is," she said. "She made a career of it. And in a man's world with mostly male chefs!"

"I know," Elaine said. "And maybe my mother knows, too. But at heart she hates the idea of my getting married someday and being the one in the kitchen who does the cooking. She wants different things for me."

"That's crazy," muttered Lucida, shaking her head. "And I thought having two mothers was nutty. Moms would be thrilled if I was good at anything, practically. Your mother should be proud. We're going to win our own cable-access program because of you!"

Elaine smiled a little. Then she stiffened and said, "Of course I am indifferent to my mother's position at this point."

"Indifferent," Lucida repeated, grinning wryly at Elaine. "Sure. Look, if I were you, I'd be having a conversation with my mother up in that office of hers. But that's just me." Lucida swung her legs over the edge of the bed. "Listen," she said. "I've been meaning to ask you this for a while. What do you keep in that chest at the foot of your bed?"

Elaine stood up and walked in front of the chest. She blocked it with her legs, turning slightly pink.

"Nothing," she said.

"Come on," Lucida said. "I've been wondering what's in that chest since the first time I came over. It's so neat-looking—the stained wood with those brass handles. It looks like an old sea chest filled with buried treasure."

"I just—it's just junk."

"Yeah, sure. If I know you, Elaine, it's filled with antique cooking utensils or seventeeth-century pages on gastronomy." Lucida fished a paper clip out of her bag. "Now move away from me," she said. "I am going to pick that lock."

"No!" Elaine shouted, getting up and shoving Lucida away from the trunk so forcefully that she fell backward onto the bed.

Lucida looked up at Elaine from the bedspread. There was hurt in her eyes.

"Oh—oh—uh, gosh, I'm sorry, Lucida," Elaine said, rushing over to her friend. "My deepest apologies. Are you all right? I didn't mean to—"

Lucida got off the bed and began gathering her things together.

"I'm going home," she said. "Violence is every woman's problem."

"No—no, please, don't," said Elaine. "I am sorry. Truly I am. I shouldn't have done that."

"Who cares what you keep in your stupid chest with the cool brass handles, anyway? I wasn't really going to break into it. Not in front of you, anyway."

"If you really would like to know, I'll tell you." Elaine shrugged and took off her glasses. "But you have to promise not to tell anyone, or my brothers will make fun of me."

"Cross my heart, *mon chef*."

Elaine said, "I keep letters in there."

"Letters? To who? Like love letters? Do you have a secret admirer that you haven't told me about, Elaine? Ooh, that's so exciting. I knew you must have a secret romantic—"

"They're letters to Julia Child," Elaine admitted, looking as though someone had just tried to strangle her. "I've been writing her letters ever since I was six years old—since I learned to write, really."

Lucida stared at Elaine in profound disappointment.

"Why are you writing letters to Julia Child?" she asked.

Elaine shrugged. "I had a lot of questions, I guess. Coq au Vin isn't the easiest thing to make when you're six, you know."

Lucida put down her bag. "Oh. Oh, well." She brightened

a little. "Did she help you? What did she say when she wrote back?"

Elaine looked surprised. "Wrote back?" she asked blankly. "Oh, no, I never mailed the letters. I just keep them. They're filed by year, month, day—sometimes even by time. Occasionally I refer to them to see how I managed a recipe at a certain point in my life, say, for example, if I want to remember how much tarragon—"

"What do you mean you've never mailed them? What's the point of writing letters to somebody if they never get them?"

Elaine shrugged. "I never considered mailing them," she said.

Lucida walked across the room and put her hand on Elaine's shoulder. "Elaine," she said. "You are definitely one of the strangest people I have ever known."

"May I remind you that today you are dressed as an eighteenth-century Amish countryman?" Elaine replied.

"Seventeenth-century *Quaker*," Lucida corrected. "Did you know that Thomas Beals was famous for spreading his message throughout the entire Northwest Territory?"

They laughed.

"So you ready to bring this thing over tomorrow?"

Lucida asked, pointing to the tape on Elaine's desk.

Elaine nodded. She hesitated before speaking. "Are you nervous?" she asked. "Well, how silly of me. You never experience anxiety, of course."

"I'm more nervous than I've ever been in my entire life!" Lucida exclaimed. "Performing with you has been the hardest work I've ever done, you know, with all that trying not to be . . ."

"Trying not to be what?"

"You know. Trying not to be—to be famous. Just, you know, just kind of being—well, you know—just trying to be . . ."

"Yourself?" Elaine said.

Lucida sighed. "Yeah, myself."

"I know," said Elaine, her eyes shining. "I know."

14

Francis wrapped the videotape in plain brown paper. Chris tied a pink ribbon around it.

"Aw, c'mon," said Francis. "You make it look like they're going to a birthday party."

"I think it's pretty," said Lucida.

"You sure you don't want me to go with you guys to the station?" Francis asked. "I could ride my bike along behind you."

"For what?" asked Lucida.

"I don't know." Francis shrugged. "Protection."

"Protection from what?" Lucida asked, laughing.

"You could get mugged," said Francis, looking serious.

"What mugger would be interested in a videotape of a show called *High School Chef*?" asked Lynn.

Francis shrugged again.

Elaine's father walked into the room. His hair was combed and he was wearing socks.

"I will drive the girls," he pronounced, buttoning his jacket. "This is a momentous day."

"Oh, come on," said Lucida, looking at everyone in the kitchen. "You're making me nervous."

Mr. Hamilton looked at Elaine, who was a little pale. She clutched her brown parcel with the pink ribbon to her chest.

"You ready?" he asked.

She nodded.

"Good. Let's go."

The girls got into the car with Mr. Hamilton. He drove them down Juniper Street and Sunset Street and then Chestnut before taking a left on Main toward Kingston. Twenty minutes later, just a few blocks away from the office building, Lucida said, "You can just let us off here, Mr. Hamilton."

"Here? You've still got a few blocks to go. I'll take you right to the door."

"No," Lucida said, glancing at Elaine. "The deadline is two o'clock. We're early. Besides, it will be nice for us to clear our heads in that little park before going in. We'll be fine."

Mr. Hamilton nodded. He pulled to the side of a little clearing with a cluster of evergreen trees shadowing a few park benches. Twenty feet away was a large parking lot; beyond that, the square office building housing WKTV. Mr. Hamilton got out of the car and hugged the girls.

"I'm proud of you both," he said.

The girls walked past a clump of trees and headed toward a bench on a path covered with pine needles. They had time, so they walked slowly. A breeze moved through the leaves.

"Do you think we should have redone the scene with the wine reduction?" Elaine asked as they walked to the bench. "I feel I may have rushed the explanation."

Lucida shrugged. "Nah. The judges will be forgiving. After all, you aren't a chef yet."

Elaine nodded. They walked a little farther into the trees, past a bench. Lucida sat down on the root of an oak.

"Will we have to speak with an executive of some kind?" Elaine asked Lucida, sitting down on the bench across from the tree root. "I would be very nervous to speak with an executive, I think."

"I doubt it. WKTV is a small outfit. We'll probably just leave it with someone at the front—"

At that moment both girls noticed a figure walking toward them. At first it was difficult to tell who it was, but gradually they realized the person heading in their direction, tall and handsome in a black cowboy hat and boots with spurs, was none other than Croton Harmon. Both girls stiffened.

"I saw you get dropped off," Croton said. There was a red bandanna around his neck. He wore a suede jacket with fringes.

"What are you doing here, Croton?" said Lucida. She scowled at him.

"Same as you, I reckon," said Croton. He lifted his cowboy hat and ran his fingers through his hair. Elaine noticed his brow was beaded with sweat.

Lucida got up and brushed off her skirt. "Well, we'd love to stay and chat," she said, looking at Elaine, who stood frozen in front of the park bench, "but we've got to hurry home to take out the garbage, right, Elaine?" She moved away from the tree.

"Wait a minute," Croton said, holding up both his hands

and moving toward them. He looked at Elaine, who looked back at him fully in the face, up close and personal, for the second time in her life. Her heart seized when she looked into his one cold eye, the cloudy eye of a dead fish, the eye of a person who was a rotten fig, a flower gone to seed.

"What do you want, Croton?"

"I want to talk."

"We don't have anything to say to you," Lucida said, trying to walk past him, but he moved quickly, blocking her movement. Elaine's eyes widened and she drew in her breath.

"Wait a minute," Croton said. He reached forward and took hold of Lucida's arm.

"Let go of me!" Lucida shrieked. Croton fixed his eyes on Elaine, noticing the parcel she was clutching.

"That's your submission, isn't it?" he said to Elaine. Still holding Lucida's arm with one hand, he removed his hat with the other and wiped his forehead with the back of his sleeve. He replaced his hat.

Elaine nodded.

"Let go of me or I'll scream!"

"I've seen an awful lot of you lately," Croton said as Lucida struggled to free her arm. "Hanging around with Lucida."

Croton let go of Lucida's arm and stepped between the girls.

"Can I see it?" he asked Elaine, holding out his hand for the brown paper parcel. He took it from her, gently.

"Are you crazy?" Lucida shouted at Elaine, attempting to get past Croton. "What are you just handing it to him for?"

Croton walked over to the root of the oak tree and sat down. He removed his hat and put it on the ground beside him. He untied the ribbon and slid the tape out of the brown paper package. He read the label on the front and took a long, deep breath, holding the tape with both hands.

"Original," he said after a long moment, nodding at Elaine and touching the tape with the tips of his fingers.

"Better than anything you could come up with on your own," Lucida said. "Now give it back."

"I know how you found out about this competition," Croton said, standing up with his hat and putting it back on. "Even though the ad in the *New Paltz Carrier* only went out just over a month ago." He was still holding the tape.

Lucida crossed her arms and glared at Croton. Elaine looked at her shoes.

"I knew you were up to something when I saw the video recorder signed out in your name at the media lab," Croton said to Lucida. "But I couldn't figure out how you knew about the competition. I had to do some serious thinking—"

Lucida snorted.

"Go ahead, make fun," Croton said, and the pupil in his cloudy eye flared. "I thought about it for some time," he continued, touching the red bandanna at his throat and turning away from the girls, facing the horizon beyond WKTV. The breeze rustled through the fringes in his jacket. "And then one night," Croton said, "I decided to do what I always do when I can't figure something out." He looked at the girls.

"I cleaned my room," he said.

"Oh, how fascinating, Croton," said Lucida. "Do tell us what kind of varnish you use on your dresser set."

"I dusted," Croton said. "I polished and I vacuumed. And just as I was about to give up trying to figure things out, I found this." Croton reached into the pocket of his jeans and held up a lipstick. It was bright orange, with little pink hearts around the plastic holder.

"Sherbet Sunrise," Elaine whispered to herself.

Croton's darker eye widened savagely, like a wild

animal. He gritted his teeth. Then he brought his thumb to his mouth and bit his fingernail.

"Why'd you do it, Lucida? You had no right to break and enter my house, to eavesdrop, to go through my things. Even worse, you had no right to falsify documents"—and here Croton reached into his pocket again and took out a crumpled piece of paper. It was, of course, the letter Elaine and Lucida had written.

"Um," said Lucida. She shot Elaine a helpless glance.

Croton looked at the videotape in his hand again. He looked troubled.

"Wasn't it enough humiliation to have me dress up like a geisha and wait around at the coffee shop for theater people who never showed up? Did you really need to double your revenge by heating up the competition at WKTV?"

Lucida bit her lip. "You embarrassed me first," she said.

"No, you embarrassed *me* first. At the Festival on the Green."

Elaine stared at her tape, still in Croton's hands. She looked at her watch. It was only a few minutes before two o'clock.

"You think people with great looks don't have problems,"

said Croton. "Well, you're wrong about that, Lucida. I've got plenty of worries. Just like anyone else."

"Maybe," Lucida conceded. "But you're weak, Croton. I have looked in your eyes and seen into your soul, and you are a rotten fig at heart, a flower gone to seed."

Croton didn't try to argue. He nodded, solemnly, moving closer to Lucida and pulling her close to him, suddenly.

"Hey! Let go of me!"

Croton put his hands on either side of Lucida's face.

"I'm going to do something bad," he whispered softly, stroking her hair as Lucida looked into his face and bit her lip again. "And what I'm going to do is a terrible thing, but I can't help it, because you're right. I am weak, as you say." Still holding Lucida's face gingerly, he kissed her forehead. At first Lucida struggled, but then Croton put his arms all the way around her, and Lucida, in a weakened state due to Croton's extreme handsomeness, slid one arm around his waist and lifted her other hand to the back of his neck, knocking off his hat and running her fingers through his black hair.

"Oh, Croton, I detest you," Lucida sighed, beating his shoulderblades as he pressed his lips to hers. The breeze gently lifted her purple feather boa.

Croton pulled away from Lucida so abruptly that she fell. Then, in one swift move, he pulled apart the plastic lid and ripped out a strip of the magnetic ribbon inside the videotape. He pulled out more ribbon, and kept on pulling, until the tape was empty and the path at their feet was covered with long strands of ribbon and bits of broken plastic.

Lucida watched from the ground in stunned silence.

Elaine's eyes filled with tears.

"I'm sorry," Croton said, handing the empty cassette to Elaine. "But you don't understand—you don't know how important it is to fulfill . . ." He trailed off.

". . . your secret wish, your life's ambition," Elaine said, quietly, to the leaves around her feet.

Croton nodded. "I can't help myself," he said. "I'm—I'm—"

A rotten fig, Elaine thought. A flower gone to seed.

"We're even now," Croton said to Lucida, replacing his hat. He adjusted his red bandanna.

"Not by a long shot!" Lucida screamed. "This is just the beginning!"

Croton looked over at Elaine. He shrugged his shoulders. Then he turned his back on the girls and walked away, disappearing quickly first into the trees, then the parking lot, then into the horizon beyond the brick building that was WKTV.

Lucida got up. She stared at the pile of ripped tape at their feet. There was an extremely long silence.

"You kissed him," Elaine half whispered.

"You gave him our videotape!" Lucida shouted.

"I—I was nervous," Elaine admitted. "I didn't know he would—"

"We don't have a backup!"

"I know," said Elaine. She shrugged her shoulders. "Come on, let's go home," she said.

Lucida stuffed a few strands of the tape ribbon into her beaded change purse. She paced around the tree. As she paced she grew angrier and angrier.

"This is all your fault," she shouted at Elaine.

"My fault?"

"Yes! You could have stopped him! You had plenty of time while he was holding me in his arms to race over and grab the tape back. You could have nabbed and raced! Now look at us! We're ruined!"

Elaine, who had never raced or nabbed in her life, stared at Lucida.

"I'd have been afraid," she began.

"Well, of course!" Lucida snapped. "You're afraid of

everything! You're afraid to talk to people. You're afraid to take risks. You're afraid to take chances, to show your face to the world!"

Elaine didn't say anything.

"I can't believe this! We worked for hours and days and weeks and for what? So you can stand by when Croton shows up and just let him ruin our only tape! This was our one chance, Elaine! Our one chance! And now it's gone!" She sat down on the root of the tree and sobbed.

"Say something!" Lucida shouted, in between sobs.

Elaine didn't know what to say.

"We're ruined, ruined!"

"It's all right."

"No, it's not," Lucida said. She stood up and collected her purse and feather boa. She wiped off her hands. She regarded Elaine coldly.

"You know what I think?" she said, after a moment.

Elaine looked at her friend, her heart sinking.

"I think you're a coward," she said. "I think you didn't really want a show in the first place, that's what I think. I bet there's a part of you that's relieved Croton busted our tape."

Elaine said nothing.

"I can't work with this," Lucida went on. She shook her head.

"I'm sorry," Elaine murmured, looking down at the path.

Lucida straightened her wig.

"I'm sorry, too," she said angrily. "You don't know how sorry I am." She looked at Elaine. "You could really be somebody. But I can't be the only one who believes in you, Elaine. You have to believe in yourself."

Lucida tossed her purple hair over her shoulder and walked away in the same direction that Croton had left. She left Elaine in the middle of the path, a pile of plastic pieces at her feet. Elaine sighed. She sighed and shrugged, and then she turned around and headed back the other way, in the direction of home.

Part Two

Dear Julia,

If she won't speak to me at school, and she won't answer my phone calls, how can we ever be friends again?

Sincerely,
Lucida Sans

15

It was a Sunday afternoon, the day of the Spring Festival on the Square. Mrs. Hamilton was standing in her usual place by the mayor and other members of the town council. The entrance was festooned with its customary balloons and flowers, and as usual, Mrs. Hamilton was greeting citizens and asking them to vote on a local proposition. The usual exhibitors and vendors lined the perimeter of the grounds, with the exception of a petting zoo, which a local farmer had set up in the middle of the square as a way of honoring the coming of spring. Chickens and geese strutted behind the fenced enclosure, bothering the piglets.

"Spring at last," said Chris. "And here we are again, stuck at the constituency table."

Francis looked around. "Where are the twins? They're not getting away with not passing out pamphlets this year. They're plenty old enough."

"Over there," said Chris. "Waiting in line to feed the lamb."

Elaine gazed longingly at the nearby booth with vertical bands of blue, white, and red going around the familiar canopy. In their usual place at the counter, Gerard Etienne was doing another cooking demonstration with his son, Marceau. Elaine sighed.

"What are they making this time?" Francis asked.

"*Steak au poivre*," said Elaine. "Shh."

Marceau held the bottle of cognac over the meat and smiled for the crowds as he poured the alcohol into the chafing dish.

"That's dangerous," Elaine told her brothers. "Fire can leap up—"

"We know, we know," Chris said.

Gerard Etienne lit a match, and the sauce around the steak burst into flames. The audience applauded. Elaine sighed again.

"Let's go see if that steak is as good as yours," Chris said.

"Yeah, let's," said Francis. The boys walked away, leaving Elaine alone at the table with the pamphlets. She sighed again. Her mother appeared.

"Elaine," she said. "I don't see you greeting anyone."

"No one has stopped by," Elaine answered.

Elaine's mother was wearing a glen-plaid suit, with sling-back heels. She looked distracted.

"Where are your brothers?"

Elaine shrugged. She looked past her mother, beyond the Jus Lié booth, to an old water tower at the top of the hill. A man was climbing a tall ladder to the top. Below him, another worker maneuvered the arm of a crane from inside a truck.

". . . as I said, Elaine, please try and look presentable. Tuck in your shirt. Where is your father? Oh, there's the mayor again. I've got to speak to him about that city park bill." Mrs. Hamilton looked back at Elaine.

"Try and represent this family with pride, all right, Elaine? For me?"

Elaine nodded, and her mother walked away. Elaine was about to take a few steps closer to Jus Lié when she noticed in the middle of the fairgrounds, to her greatest surprise, none other than Lucida Sans and Croton Harmon. Lucida was dressed in regular clothing, although she still wore her favorite wig, and she was carrying a megaphone. Croton, in black tights and a painted white face, practiced breaking his way out of an imaginary box while Lucida assembled lights and set up the tripod of a videotape camera. Both of them were too busy to notice that Elaine was watching from a short distance away.

"He looks ridiculous, doesn't he?" said Chris, from behind Elaine with a paper plate of *steak au poivre*.

"What's Lucida doing with him?" Francis wanted to know.

It had been a few months since Elaine had spoken to Lucida, of course, but she had noticed her hanging around Croton at school, helping him produce his winning television show on the cable-access channel at WKTV.

"Where have you been?" said Chris. "They're together again. Except everyone knows he only pretends to like her so she can help him produce his show."

Francis nodded, looking unhappy. He watched as Lucida followed Croton around the fairground, struggling to balance the video camera on her shoulder as he pretended to interview some children with an imaginary microphone.

"We would have won," Francis said quietly.

"Oh, Lucida!" Chris called in a high voice, his mouth full of steak. "We're over here! With the people who like you for who you are!"

"Be quiet, Chris," said Elaine.

But Lucida, who was struggling to hold the camera in one hand and a clipboard in the other, turned abruptly in the direction of Chris's voice, lost her balance, and fell backward into a woman who was leaning over her daughter at the gate of the petting zoo. The mother, who had been about to transfer a handful of grain to her child, also lost her balance and fell, knocking a fistful of feed onto the ground beside the gate separating the children from the animals.

What happened next is hard to describe. The baby lamb hopped over the fence in search of the feed, startling some chickens and a few piglets. The gander flapped his wings and honked his disapproval, which panicked the lamb, causing him to notice that he was no longer protected by the safety of his zoo enclosure. Within moments, he had run through the entrance and out onto the street.

"Lamb's out!" cried the farmer. Children and their parents, vendors and exhibitors, and even the mayor looked up to see what the hubbub was about. Meanwhile, the lamb was trying to dodge the oncoming traffic on either side of the roadway. A truck screeched on its brakes, and the car behind the truck flew into its rear. A van behind the car swerved to the right and crossed over the median strip, running into a wagon heading down the road in the other direction. Cars and trucks and vans ran into one another in both lanes, creating an amazing pileup that went on for nearly half a mile. An eighteen-wheeler heading down the road from a distance noticed the wreck and threw his cab into reverse to avoid another collision — which would have been a brilliant move had he noticed the crane at the foot of the hill by the water tower.

"What the—" muttered the crane operator, as his hand on the lever was knocked to one side by the force of the hit. The boom swung violently into the wooden legs holding up the platform of the water tower, which groaned and rocked back and forth, threatened to buckle, and then, amazingly, held itself steady.

"You all right up there?" the crane operator called to his signalman, getting out of his truck and looking up the ladder leading to the platform of the water tower.

The man on the platform gave the crane operator a thumbs-up. He took off his cap and wiped the sweat off his brow. The crane operator let out his breath.

There was a funny creaking sound followed by a

thunderous crash as the legs beneath the platform of the water tower gave way.

"Look out!" cried the man on the ladder, leaping into a haystack as the tank exploded open and thousands of tons of water poured down the hill in a gigantic wave heading straight for the Festival on the Square. The wave knocked over the exhibition tents and vendor stands and leveled the gate penning in the farm animals. Water sloshed through the square, carrying with it a sea of ice-cream cones and paper plates, town councilmen and farmyard animals. Pigs and chickens bobbed and floated above the fairground like plastic toys in a child's bathtub. The whole thing took place in less than ten seconds.

Amazingly, no one at the New Paltz Spring Festival on the Square was seriously hurt. The fire department came, the police showed up, and of course the local news arrived in their signature white vans. Lucida Sans swam up to a reporter in order to answer some questions while Chris and Francis went to look for their mother and the twins. The reporter happened to be conducting his interview right by the constituency table where Elaine, who had not moved, was standing waist deep in a river of soggy pamphlets. Lucida caught her staring. Elaine looked away.

"What's it to you?" Lucida said, looking annoyed. She took off her feather boa, which was wilted and drenched, and dropped it into the water. It floated away like a river snake.

Elaine began collecting her mother's pamphlets.

"It wasn't my fault," said Lucida. She bent down and felt around in the water until she came up with the broken handle of the video camera. She examined it for a moment before shrugging and tossing it back into the water.

"Oh, but it was," Elaine said, her eyes wide with admiration. "It was."

"What do you know about it?" Lucida demanded.

Elaine shrugged.

Lucida sloshed her way over to Elaine. She scowled at her.

"Why haven't you returned any of my calls?" Lucida asked.

"Why are you hanging around with *him*?" asked Elaine, pointing across the water to the roof of a portable toilet booth, where Croton was emptying water from his shoe while the lamb chewed on a handkerchief sticking out of his breast pocket. Croton gave Elaine and Lucida a terrible look.

"I know," Lucida admitted. She shrugged. "But he's handsome, anyway."

"I have to go," Elaine said. She fished the last pamphlet out of the water and stuffed it into a plastic bag. "I've got to find my family."

Lucida stared at Elaine and bit her lip. Elaine moved to go, but Lucida took her arm as she was about to wade past.

"Listen, Elaine," said Lucida. "I've been trying to tell you all this time, I didn't mean—"

"Yes, you did," Elaine said. She took off her glasses and looked at Lucida. She shrugged. "You're right, anyway. I guess I am a coward."

"I was just angry," Lucida began, but Elaine replaced her glasses and waded away in the direction of the entrance.

"Fine," Lucida called after her, peeling strands of her sopping wig away from her cheek. "Be that way."

Elaine kept going in the direction of the entrance, where she knew her family would be waiting for her. She didn't look back.

Dear Julia,

For the past few months I have devoted my energies to making bread, as it keeps my mind from other problems. Obstacles to producing a proper crust will not deter me from my goal. After all, when the famous cook and teacher Madeleine Kamman told her students to destroy their copies of *Mastering the Art of French Cooking*, you said, good for her for being so ambitious.

I will try not to be fearful in the face of adversity. I will try to be ambitious.

Yours,

Elaine Hamilton

P.S. I attempted three omelettes yesterday evening. All failed. The first would not dislodge from the pan, the second rolled into a cylinder too tight to be deemed attractive, and the third, though lovely on one side, was unacceptably brown on the other.

16

Elaine improved her knife skills and experimented with different brands of yeast. She read about brick ovens and made bar graphs illustrating the various effects of temperature on rising dough. She made loaves of *pain de Boulanger, pain doré, pain dur, pain brié*. She made *pain de champagne, pain complet, pain long, pain de mie*. She made *pain quotidien*. She baked *pain d'épices*, a spicy delicious gingerbread sprinkled with sugar. She made *pain de sucre, pain de son,* even *un petit pain*. And in between loaves she continued to teach whoever happened to be in the kitchen—usually the twins—the proper technique and practice necessary to achieve culinary success.

"You want to cut a very deep slit," she told Robyn and Leslie, poised over their chickens at the counter, gripping the handles of their sharpened blades. "A deep slit," she went on, "down the back of the bird from the neck to the tail, in order to expose the backbone. Always cut against the bone so as to avoid piercing the skin."

"I doubt I would win reelection," Mrs. Hamilton remarked one afternoon as Robyn and Leslie turned their turkey carcasses at the breastbone, "if anyone knew our six-year-olds were handling a deboning knife on our kitchen counter."

"But, ah, the agility," Mr. Hamilton noted, shaking his head in amazement. "No marring of the flesh, no gashes, no slashes, not so much as a nick." He tilted his head to the side and gazed at the boys, then back at Elaine. "Only the finest teacher could train small hands like that."

"You know," said Chris some weeks later, as Elaine guided Robyn in the filleting of a Dover sole, "you really are a patient teacher." Francis watched as Leslie discarded the tiny bones and separated the skin from the flesh.

"Imagine if you could teach the world to fillet a sole like that, not just a couple of runny-nosed first graders," Chris mused, shaking his head. "Such a shame."

Elaine slammed the oven door shut, nearly burning herself as she placed a loaf pan on the cooling rack.

The aroma of the bread wafted around the kitchen, and Mr. Hamilton, passing by the kitchen door in his now tight-fitting yoga bodysuit on the way to the basement, smelled the crusty loaf and groaned, and hefted his weight, and knew that he would have to eat it.

"I saw her again today," Chris whispered to Francis at the kitchen table when Elaine had turned on the mixer.

Francis nodded. "Me, too," he said.

Elaine went upstairs to get a cookbook.

"I don't get it," said Francis.

"Get what?"

"Why she lets him use her like that."

"The powers of attraction are mysterious," Chris said, unfolding the ironing board.

"He's terrible," said Francis.

"He's handsome," said Chris.

"He shaves his chest hair," said Francis in disgust. "Marty saw him do it in the locker room."

Chris shook his head. "I understand Lucida," he said, licking his finger and touching the bottom of the iron. "Being around Croton Harmon makes you feel important."

"You do know," said Francis, "it's because of Mr.

Handsome Harmon that Elaine makes nine loaves of French bread before seven thirty every morning."

Chris sighed and nodded. "I miss Lucida," he said. "I miss her beaded scarf and that yellow wig with the rhinestones braided into it. She used to let me borrow it whenever I wanted."

"I just miss *her*," said Francis, and a funny look came into his eyes.

"Maybe there's something we could do," said Chris.

"Like what?"

"I don't know. Something. Before Elaine buries herself in a mountain of unbleached flour and never comes out."

"Before Dad has to go to the fat farm," added Francis.

Elaine returned to the kitchen with a stack of cookbooks and three balloon whisks.

"What about that contest posted in the *New Paltz Carrier*?" said Chris.

"What contest?"

"You know," said Chris. "The one about the cooking competition."

"I never heard anything about that," Francis said. "Why didn't you tell me about that before?"

Chris shrugged. "I didn't think Elaine would go for

it." He got up and fished a newspaper out of the trash. "Here, look."

Francis looked at the paper for a moment. Elaine left the twins boning fish at the counter and went back upstairs to her room. Chris and Francis looked at each other and got up from the table.

"If you don't mind," Elaine told Chris and Francis as they came into her room. "I am busy." She tore the page out of the notebook she was writing in and crumpled it into a ball.

"We have to talk to you," Chris said.

"Yeah," Francis said. "It's urgent."

Elaine put down her pencil and took off her glasses.

"What?" she said.

"We read something in the *New Paltz Carrier* we thought you should see," Chris said, kicking off his red pumps. He sat down on the edge of Elaine's bed and fanned out his dress a little.

"We thought you'd find it interesting," said Francis.

Elaine took the paper from Francis and looked at it.

"So?" Elaine said. She tossed the paper on the bed and picked up her pencil. "CSNY sponsors the Young Chef's Competition every year."

"We think you should sign up. We think you can win."

"No, thank you. I'm not interested in cooking competitions."

"Listen, Elaine," Francis said, glancing at Chris, who nodded at him. "Chris and I have been talking. We know that you and"—he looked over at Chris again, who motioned that he should continue—"and Lucida aren't talking and all that. But maybe now would be a good time to—to patch things up."

Elaine put her glasses back on and opened a cookbook. Francis shrugged his shoulders and looked back at Chris.

"Go on," Chris whispered. Francis stood up.

"We think you're a great cook. And you and Lucida were a great team. You could pair up with her and win. Chris and I could help out if you wanted."

"Yeah, Elaine," said Chris. "We'd help you."

"I'm not interested in competitive cooking," Elaine replied. "It's all flair and showmanship."

"But look what it says here," said Francis, picking up the paper again and reading from it. "'Contestants will prepare a three-course French meal using items from a market basket. Points are awarded on the basis of presentation, organization, and'—listen to this, Elaine—'explanation.'"

Elaine looked at Chris, puzzled.

"Why explanation?" she asked.

Chris stood up and waved the paper around. "That's just it, Elaine," he said. "The winner gets to audition for a show on *network television*. They send the winner to New York City to—"

"I don't want my own television show."

"Yeah, but Lucida does," said Chris, starting to look excited. "And you know what else it says here?" Chris went on. "The winner also gets a free scholarship to a cooking school in Paris. It's a two-year program, I think. Isn't that great? Didn't you say you always wanted to go to a cooking school?"

Elaine turned her back on her brothers and looked at the photograph of Julia Child slicing mushrooms on the wall by the window.

"Does the paper say," she asked, quietly, still looking at the photograph, "does it happen to mention which school they are offering a scholarship to?"

Francis looked at Chris. He shrugged and picked up the paper. He squinted at the words.

"Some school called—" He squinted again. "Something called the Cord—"

"The Cordon Bleu," Elaine repeated softly.

"Yeah," Francis said. He looked up. "Have you heard of it?"

At that moment Robyn and Leslie walked in with a platter of Sole Meunière. Leslie handed Elaine a fork while Robyn set the platter on her desk. Elaine forked up a bit of the fish and tasted it. She nodded.

"You didn't brown the butter for long enough," she said. "But the texture is excellent. Did you fillet the other fish?"

"Yes."

"Good. I'll teach you how to make Sole Bonne Femme in a minute."

"Don't waste this opportunity," Chris said after the twins had gone. "This isn't some cable-access show with bad lighting. This is national. You'd be the first teenager to teach young people how to cook. Millions of young people. Plus the scholarship in Paris, besides."

"You'd be famous, Elaine," said Francis.

"I don't want to be famous," said Elaine.

"You could start your own school," Chris said. "The Elaine Hamilton School for the Culinary Arts."

Elaine looked like she was thinking this over.

"I don't think so," she said finally. "Although it does sound tempting. The idea that I could reach so many aspiring chefs." She paused a moment, tapping her pencil on the desk. "I'm not comfortable in front of the camera," she said. "I'd be afraid."

"No, you wouldn't," said Chris. "You just need another shot, that's all."

Elaine shook her head. "Honestly, I just don't think I could handle that kind of pressure."

"At least think about it," Chris said.

"Please, Elaine," said Francis.

But Elaine had already turned away from her brothers. She pushed her glasses up closer to her face and leaned over a recipe, running her finger down the page. The conversation was over.

17

"You must learn to interact with the male gender," Mrs. Hamilton said to Elaine in the car as they exited the highway, turning onto a winding road on the way to Dartmouth College. Giant trees bordered the roadside, their leaves swaying in the wind as Mrs. Hamilton whizzed by. Cows grazed on distant hilltops.

"When I graduated in seventy-six," Elaine's mother continued, her hands on the steering wheel as she looked out at the greenery, "the political atmosphere was charged. We stood at the helm of the women's liberation movement."

Elaine nodded and looked out the window.

"We played a crucial role in history," Mrs. Hamilton

said. "Now it's your turn, as next in the line of Hamilton descendants, to carry the torch." She glanced sideways. "Are you listening to me, Elaine?"

"Yes," Elaine answered.

"It's your birthright to attend Dartmouth," her mother said.

"What if I don't get in?" Elaine asked.

"Then you'll go to a safety school."

"The guidance counselor says that Princeton and Yale are not traditional safety schools," Elaine said.

The motor thrummed as the car shifted into a lower gear on a hill.

"You'll get in," Mrs. Hamilton said quickly, glancing sideways at Elaine again and patting her leg. "Don't worry about that, sweetheart. Dartmouth is a Hamilton family tradition."

Mrs. Hamilton drove the car up Wheelock Street, past the cafés and restaurants on Main until they came to Dartmouth Green, a large square crisscrossed with paths and benches. A few students tossed a Frisbee back and forth across the lawn. It was a beautiful day, bright and green, warm with summer.

Mrs. Hamilton parked the car on Main Street. Elaine clutched the leather folder her mother had given her as a present. It contained pamphlets about the college as well as the application, which her mother said she might want to carry around, just in case she felt like filling it out at the library after the interview. They crossed the green. Mrs. Hamilton smiled at the passing students on bicycles and pointed out Dartmouth Hall and the library spire.

"Isn't it picturesque?" she sighed.

Elaine nodded. She thought of the photos she had seen of the town center in Northampton, the little hill leading up the main street to the filigreed gate that welcomed students to the campus of Smith College, which Julia Child had attended from 1930 to 1934.

"The women's studies building is that way," Mrs. Hamilton was saying, pointing behind the clock tower. "In Carpenter Hall. Of course it didn't exist when I was there. But we paved the way for gender studies. I'm sure you will build on that tradition."

"Do they offer courses in French literature?" Elaine asked. Julia Child had taken French grammar and literature courses in her sophomore year.

"Yes, sweetheart," Mrs. Hamilton said vaguely. She looked up brightly. "Oh, look, there's Webster! Look at those lovely columns. We organized a Take Back the Night march right past Collis over there."

Elaine and her mother walked past a performing-arts center and continued down a narrow street in the direction of the administration building. Elaine's feet hurt in the shoes her mother had bought her back home. She felt hot and itched slightly in her blazer.

They came to the entrance of a large building with tall windows. Mrs. Hamilton looked at her watch.

"We're still twenty minutes early for your interview," she said. "Would you like to sit on the green for a little while? We could go over your talking points."

"I guess," said Elaine. They went to a bench and sat down.

"Please don't slouch in the interview, Elaine. You have a tendency to hunch over when you're nervous."

Elaine nodded.

"What will you say when they ask about your extracurricular activities?"

"I passed out pamphlets at the women's convention in Chicago," Elaine replied. "I campaigned for shelter improvements in low-income areas."

"Honestly, Elaine, can you try to sound a little more enthusiastic? You might as well be in a coma."

"I'll try."

"Speak in complete sentences."

"All right."

Mrs. Hamilton looked at the trees and the students throwing the Frisbee and sighed again.

"Look, Elaine," she said. "Maybe Dartmouth is not your first choice for a school. Don't think I'm not aware of this. I know in some ways you might prefer to attend some other college—Princeton, Yale—"

Smith, the Cordon Bleu, Elaine thought.

"—but you'll soon understand that this is a wonderful atmosphere for you to develop as an individ—"

"Mrs. Fischburger Number One went to Wellesley," Elaine said, softly.

"Who is Mrs. Fischburger Number One?"

"One of Lucida's mothers."

"Oh, yes," Mrs. Hamilton said. She paused thoughtfully. "It's not that I mean to condemn the well-meaning feminists who feel strongly about women's colleges. For some women this is an important path. But not for you, Elaine. You need to learn to live among men."

"But I do live among them," Elaine said, thinking of Francis, Chris, Lynn, Robyn, and Leslie.

"Yes, but your voice must rise above the others," said Mrs. Hamilton. "Who will hear you at a women's college? Feminists attending women's schools are preaching to the choir." She looked at Elaine with love and admiration.

"You're so gifted," she said, stroking her daughter's hair. "I'm so proud of your test scores and your transcripts. I couldn't have asked for a more hardworking daughter. I want every opportunity made available to you. It's difficult to maintain a position in government."

"But I don't want a position in government," Elaine said.

"What's that, my love?"

Elaine shook her head.

A pair of young girls in sandals and handkerchiefs approached the bench where Elaine and her mother were sitting. One was tall and thin, and the other was plump. They had earnest faces and smelled of patchouli.

"Excuse me," said the earnest-looking thin one. "I don't mean to be rude, but, are you—are you Elizabeth Hamilton, the United States congresswoman?"

"Yes! What a pleasure to be recognized."

"Wow. I mean, we're studying your speeches in Gender and the Law. We think ratifying the Equal Rights Amendment is so, like, cool!"

"Can I have your autograph?" the plump one asked.

Mrs. Hamilton took out a pen and the girls held out their notebooks.

"This is my daughter, Elaine," Mrs. Hamilton said, signing and putting the cap back on her pen. "She'll be taking freshman courses in the women's studies department. Maybe she'll even be in a few classes with you two young women!"

"Hi," said the girls.

"We'd be happy to show you around," said the thin one. "We'd be so honored."

"Elaine?"

"Thank you," Elaine mumbled.

The girls squinted in the sunlight at Elaine. There was a long silence.

"Well . . . it was very nice to meet you," they said, backing away a little.

"There," Mrs. Hamilton said as the girls wandered off. "You see? You have friends already." She stood up and looked at her watch.

"It's time," she said.

The admissions officer was a tall man with a white mustache and silvery blue eyes. There was an aroma of fine tobacco about him, and he wore a bow tie. On his desk were stacks of papers, a cigar still wrapped in cellophane, and a thick manila folder with Elaine's name on it.

"Elaine Hamilton," he said with delight. He shook her hand and motioned for her to sit down across from him. The office was small, and the admission officer's legs were so long their knees practically touched. "I'm William Allen Nelson," he said.

Elaine nodded and tried to smile.

"It's nice to meet you," she said politely.

"Yes. Well! I've looked over your transcripts, and the committee has reviewed your test scores." Mr. Nelson leaned over the desk against the wall, picked up his cigar, and put it in his mouth, even though it was still wrapped in plastic. "I see no reason," he continued, putting down the cigar, "given your academic standing and your family's contribution—the Hamilton wing in the engineering building, the department of women's studies, the new gymnasium, the botanical gardens—that you don't stand a *considerably* good chance of getting into this institution." He tossed the folder on the desk and leaned back in his chair. "I'm sure you have many interests that can be met here at Dartmouth," he said, smiling pleasantly.

Elaine nodded.

"For example, we have world-renowned science departments. Are you interested in pursuing a career in the sciences?"

Elaine shook her head.

"Ah, an arts major perhaps? We have a wonderful art school—"

"No, no, thank you," Elaine said. "Sir."

"What about mathematics? Your scores were among the highest in your class."

Elaine shook her head again.

"Our country's next modern novelist, perhaps?" Mr. Nelson ran his thumb and index finger down the length of his white mustache. The edges of his face were creased with smile lines.

"Julia Child thought about becoming a novelist," Elaine said. She gasped. She had only meant to think the words.

"Excuse me?"

"Nothing," Elaine said, horrified. "I was—I mean, I—I'm sorry."

"Sorry? About what? Did I hear you say something about Julia Child?

"You did say Julia Child," he repeated, scratching his head.

Elaine looked at Mr. Nelson's shoes. "I guess I did," she whispered.

The man studied Elaine for a few moments.

"If I recall," he said slowly, rolling back over to the desk and removing some papers from the manila folder, "you wrote a very long prequalification statement about the history of the equal rights movement and how you wish to play a role in it."

Elaine nodded.

"Does this have something to do with Julia Child?" he asked curiously.

"Not—not *directly*," Elaine said.

"You did write this statement, did you not?"

"Yes," Elaine said. "I wrote it."

"Hmm." He scanned a few lines, as if to refresh his memory, and tossed the pages back on the desk. He picked up the cellophane-wrapped cigar from the ashtray once more. "Excuse me," he said, pointing to the cigar. "It's an embarrassing habit, but I do so like fine things."

Elaine relaxed a little, and sat back in her chair. Mr. Nelson squinted thoughtfully at Elaine.

"You wrote the statement," he said, looking excited and sitting upright in his chair. "But it wasn't exactly your sentiment."

Elaine smiled. She nodded.

"Maybe they were your words," he went on. "But they were not precisely your—your *convictions*," he suggested, finishing the thought after a long, reflective moment. His eyes shone with delight.

"That's right," Elaine said, feeling very much understood by Mr. Nelson.

The admissions man sat up and leaned toward Elaine.

"Miss Hamilton," he asked. "May I be straightforward?"

"Of course," Elaine replied.

"Do you wish to attend Dartmouth?"

A faraway look came into Elaine's eyes. She stared off behind the desk, into the painting of the library spire behind the admissions officer's chair.

"Mr.—Mr.—"

"William Allen Nelson," he said. "Everyone calls me Will."

"Mr. . . . Will. Did you know that adding *foie gras* to about two cups of chopped game-bird meat will make a magnificent *mousseline de volaille*?"

"I happen to love a good *mousseline*," Mr. Nelson said.

"Any type of cold fowl will do. You can mix several kinds together, if you like."

Mr. Nelson's eyes lit up.

"You can add sautéed chicken livers to game meat, but if you happen to have *foie gras*, it will be more delicious."

Elaine opened her backpack and removed a small

container. Inside the container was a rolled-up plastic bag. She unrolled the plastic bag and produced a smaller bag, inside which was a frozen pack to keep everything cold. She removed a small jar of *mousseline de volaille*, a tiny spreading knife, and some crackers. She opened another bag, took out a cloth napkin, and laid it on top of the manila folder with her name on it. She put out a wedge of *Camembert*, a cluster of grapes, and two lemon tartlets.

"Do you mind?" Elaine asked.

"Not at all. Please."

Elaine spread some of the *mousseline* onto a cracker and handed it to Mr. William Allen Nelson.

He took a bite, and his white mustache moved up and down as he chewed. His silvery eyes twinkled.

"Sublime," he said, shaking his head in disbelief. "Have you made this many times?"

Elaine nodded. "Today was the three hundred and eighth time," she said, spreading some on a cracker for herself. "But today I used a few extra truffles, in spite of the expense." She chewed thoughtfully and cocked her head to one side. "I think it makes for a subtle difference in flavor," she said. "What do you think?"

"Oh, I couldn't agree more. The more truffles, the

better. May I?" he asked, reaching for another cracker.

"Of course. You may wish to try the tartlets."

Mr. William Allen Nelson closed his eyes and chewed slowly. "Extraordinary," he murmured. "Exquisite." He opened his eyes. "How old are you?"

"Sixteen."

"You don't really want to work in politics, do you?" He paused, waiting for Elaine's response. He glanced over at the last piece of *Camembert*.

"I want to be a chef," Elaine replied. "I want to attend Smith College, like Julia Child. Then I wish to attend the Cordon Bleu in Paris."

"Of course you do," answered Mr. William Allen Nelson, understanding completely.

"My mother"—Elaine lowered her voice—"she has other plans for me."

"Of course she does."

"Mr. Nelson?"

"Call me Will."

"Becoming a chef is my most cherished dream, my most secret ambition."

"Naturally. Any other vocation would be unspeakable."

Elaine leaned forward in her chair. "Do you think I'll

be able to fulfill my life's ambition?" she asked. "Without my mother or the help of Lucida Sans?"

"The computer font?" Mr. Nelson asked, looking confused.

"She wears a feather boa," said Elaine. "We aren't on speaking terms, unfortunately."

Mr. Nelson nodded soberly. "Hmm, well," he said. "You may have some things to work out with—with Lucida Sans. And your mother. Yes, I suspect you do. But I have a good feeling about this. I think with a little bravery you will be able to fulfill this cherished dream of yours, this—"

"My life's ambition."

"Your life's ambition."

"I don't want to work in the public sector," Elaine said, rather abruptly.

Mr. Nelson looked startled. Then he smiled warmly.

"You know," he said. "I don't think you'll have to. Your mother is a very smart and practical woman. Of course, I didn't vote for her when I lived in the Hudson Valley. But my wife did."

Elaine began rolling up her plastic bag and putting the containers back into her backpack.

"Be brave," Mr. Nelson said, standing up and brushing the crumbs off his lap. "Be brave and go forth. You'll always have a place here at Dartmouth if you change your mind."

"Thank you, Mr. Nelson."

"Will. Are you—will you be taking the rest of this *mousseline* with you?"

Elaine shook her head.

"Good luck to you then, Elaine Hamilton. I'll be watching out for you."

"Thank you," Elaine said. She shook the admissions officer's hand. "Thank you very much."

Dear Julia,

Okay, so Croton Harmon is truly a rotten fig and a sociopath, but at least he is willing to speak to me when his other friends are not around. Which is more than I can say for you-know-who. And Croton and I are having a perfectly wonderful time together, so I do not care if I speak to her again, really I don't.

Yours sincerely,

Lucida Sans

Dear Julia,

Did you ever think a great deal, perhaps for a long period of time, about something besides haute cuisine? Lately it seems I have so many things on my mind.

Sincerely,

Elaine Hamilton

18

It was seven thirty on a Wednesday night. Mr. Hamilton was out with the twins. Lynn was at a regional spelling bee with Mrs. Hamilton. Francis was in the backyard arguing with Chris about how to throw a baseball. Occasionally Elaine looked out the window in between putting the finishing touches on dinner.

"You can't throw a ball in a denim skirt," Francis was saying. "Go change."

"It's not denim. It's spandex. It stretches."

Elaine had nearly finished with the Filet de Boeuf en Croûte. She had stuffed and tied a Filet de Boeuf en Feuilletons Duxelles the day before. She let it sit in the refrigerator to pick up extra flavor. The *filet* had been in the oven for nearly thirty-five minutes now, and juices had just begun to escape into the pan, a sign that the meal was nearly ready.

Elaine opened the oven, letting the heat and aroma fill the kitchen.

"I don't care what material it is. It's a skirt. Get rid of it."

"I don't want to learn how to throw. Please don't make me."

Elaine removed the pastry and slid it onto the platter. Steam rose out of the *brioche*. A wonderful smell permeated the kitchen.

"I need practice fielding grounders. Start throwing."

"Girls don't play sports." Chris let out a little scream and ducked as Francis tossed the ball at him.

Elaine brought the pastry to the table and rested it on a trivet. She leaned forward on her elbows and marveled at it. She had spent hours preparing the meat the day before, cooking the brown sauce, marinating the flavors. The roast was her crowning achievement for the week.

"Girls play sports," Francis replied. "Anyway, you are *not* a girl."

"Says who?"

Elaine tossed some fresh asparagus spears in butter and opened a bottle of Bordeaux-Médoc. She got out a serving knife and cut all around the crust of the *brioche* a half inch from the bottom. She went to the kitchen window.

"Dinner's ready," she called.

"Just a second," Francis called back. "We'll be right there."

Elaine tossed a small salad with a vinaigrette dressing. She separated the slices of meat with a spoon and a fork and cut down through the bottom crust so that each slice was served with a portion of the stuffing and pastry. She spooned some of the sauce around the meat and added a piece of the top crust.

"Lean into it," Francis said. "Use the weight of your body, not just your arm."

"Look what you made me do. I got a grass stain on my pump."

"Throw the ball."

"I hate you."

"Throw it!"

A ball went through the kitchen window, knocking over the bottle of wine on the counter and bouncing into the asparagus pan. Elaine frowned.

"Not bad!" Francis said, turning his baseball cap

around on his head as he came into the kitchen. Chris followed, carrying one of his shoes.

"Look what he made me do," said Chris, pointing to the broken heel. He looked at the elaborate platter on the table surrounded by the vegetable *matignon*, the sauceboat of brown sauce, the asparagus sizzling with the baseball in it, the tipped wine bottle.

"Oh, my gosh, Elaine," said Chris. "That looks divine!"

Francis took the baseball out of the sauté pan and washed it off in the kitchen sink.

"Let me help you set the table," said Chris. "Should we use the crystal tonight? It's only Wednesday, but this dinner looks so—"

"Yes," said Elaine. "Get the crystal. And use the sterling silverware."

The boys looked at each other. Their mother only used the sterling when she had diplomats or the CEO of a company over to dinner. They weren't even sure they were allowed to use the sterling.

"I have something to say to you both," said Elaine.

Chris said, "Should I change into something formal?" He glanced at the *filet*. "Of course there might not be time to both shower and powder my—"

"Oh, for pete's sake," Francis said. Elaine removed her dish towel and took off her apron. She went to the cabinet and took out another bottle of wine—the 1927 Châteauneuf-du-Pape. She handed Francis the bottle and removed the corkscrew from the counter.

Chris kicked off his other pump and sat down at the table.

"What is it, Elaine?" asked Francis.

"I've made a decision."

The kitchen was very quiet. The butter sizzled softly in the pan. The clock ticked loudly over the stove.

"I've been thinking," Elaine said, looking above her brothers at the saucepans, the casserole dishes, the pots and ladles hanging from the iron rack above the stove. "I've been ruminating for days now, and after much concentration and consideration, I've decided—"

Francis and Chris leaned forward at the table.

"I've had a change of heart. I think I'd like to enter that competition after all."

There was a moment of silence as Chris and Francis digested Elaine's words. Then Chris jumped up, and the edge of his skirt caught on a splinter of wood beneath the table, and there was an awful ripping sound. He screamed, unsnagged his skirt, and threw his arms around his sister.

"Wow, Elaine! Oh, my gosh!"

Francis took off his cap and grinned. He wiped the sweat off the back of his neck.

"Elaine, we're going to win! You're going to cook like crazy! You'll make the most fabulous, the most amazing, the most unbelievable—"

"I was looking at the rules of the competition," Elaine said. "And while I can't say I agree with the fundamental concept of a cooking contest"—she paused—"I've decided that the scholarship prize is too tempting to pass up."

"We're gonna win, we're gonna *win*," Chris said, racing around the table, setting down the sterling silverware in a mad rush. His torn skirt hung open at the knee, but he paid no attention.

"The contest is at the end of next month, Elaine," Francis said, disentangling himself from Chris, who was jumping up and down and hugging him. "Are you sure you and Lucida can get it together in time?"

"Lucida won't be helping me this time," Elaine said.

Chris and Francis looked at each other.

"She was a great assistant," Elaine continued, taking a breath. "But I don't think our friendship can withstand . . ." Elaine trailed off, looking at the baker's rack for a moment. She took off her spectacles.

"Look," Elaine said. "If you want me to take part in this competition, you two are going to have to be my assistants. I'll need to educate you both in the fundamentals of knife skills, of garniture and presentation, of basting and sautéing, peeling and parboiling. And I'll need you to ask the important questions," she said. "Just like—like Lucida did before."

"Us?" said Francis, in surprise.

"Oh, I don't know, Elaine," said Chris. "I'm not even as good as the twins with the knife—"

"But we'll do our best," Francis cut in, glancing over at Chris. He grinned. "We'll help, Elaine. Sure we will." He opened the Châteauneuf-du-Pape and poured some for everyone. They clinked their glasses together.

"To the Hamilton family chefs," said Chris, taking a sip of his wine. "Long may we simmer, forever may we sauté. . . ."

"We better start soon," Francis said, putting down his glass of wine.

Elaine nodded. "After dinner," she said. "The contest is nine weeks away."

Dear Julia,

I greeted the morning with two omelettes: one was raw, the other scorched. That I can't master the simple omelette, Mrs. Child, is the abiding bane of my career.

You may wonder why I don't accept Lucida's calls, but why should I? Maintaining a friendship with Lucida is like baking a Charlotte Malakoff with Gravensteins. There will always be a risk of collapse. Then again, there is only a little more than two months before the competition, and Chris will have his own knife. I can't imagine a greater risk than that.

Maybe I'll speak with her when the competition has reached its conclusion. For now, I must be disciplined and maintain concentration. I must be brave.

Yours,

Elaine Hamilton

19

For nine weeks, from five thirty in the morning until eleven o'clock at night, Elaine taught Francis and Chris the fundamentals of cookery. They chopped, diced, sliced, and glazed. They creamed, puréed, strained, and emulsified. Elaine taught them the rudiments of marinades and compound butters and explained the differences between stocks and sauces, soups and consommés. Together they boiled and poached, stewed and steamed, braised and baked. They roasted, seared, sauteéd, fried, grilled, boiled, and griddled. She taught them everything she knew about *quiches* and tarts and *gratins*, *soufflés* and *crêpes* and *quenelles*. They made roasted chicken, sautéed chicken, fricasseed chicken, braised chicken. She reviewed the cold buffet, such as aspics and mousses, and taught them the elements of desserts, such as beating egg whites and the way to form a ribbon with egg yolks and sugar. She taught them how to make whipped cream and caramel and custards, Bavarian creams and mousses.

"This will have to do," she told Chris when he complained that the contest was two days away and he didn't know how to flambé.

"You can't even peel a carrot without emptying a box of Band-Aids," Francis said, wiping his forehead with the edge of his apron. "Now you want to set fire to cognac?"

Elaine had to admit that their time was up, that they would have to make do with whatever they had learned.

"Don't worry," she said, although she herself was worried. Francis was slumped at the kitchen table, surrounded by fluted mushrooms. Chris's curly locks were limp from vegetable oil. The kitchen was a mess of melting butter and heavy cream and blanched almonds from a lesson in pastry.

Mrs. Hamilton came downstairs and looked in the kitchen. She frowned.

"It's eleven thirty," she said. "Time to clean up."

"Mom?" Chris said, standing up and pushing his hair out of his eyes. There was almond cream in his hair. Six of his ten fingers had Band-Aids on them. "The contest is the day after tomorrow. Will you be there?"

"You know I can't, Christopher. I have a convention at city hall. I'm meeting with the committee for gender equality in the morning, and then I have a meeting with the mayor in the afternoon."

"But we've been slaving over a hot stove for weeks," said Chris.

Mrs. Hamilton glanced at Elaine, who was wiping the counter.

"That's precisely what I'm trying to get Elaine to avoid," said Mrs. Hamilton as if Elaine were not in the room. Mrs. Hamilton turned around to leave.

"Well, wait, Mom," Christopher persisted. "Aren't you at least going to wish Elaine good luck? It's a *national* competition, after all."

"Shut the hell up, Chris," Francis said.

"It's all right," Elaine said. "She doesn't have to wish me luck. It takes more than luck to win these competitions anyway." She turned on the faucet at the sink and dampened the edge of a dish towel.

Mrs. Hamilton spoke to Francis. "Elaine knows," she

said, "that I wish her all the luck in the world in any pursuit she chooses. But I cannot in good faith stand by and let her ruin her future by attending some cooking school in Paris, no more than I can permit her to attend a women's college. It defies everything I stand for, all that our family has worked toward."

"You don't suppose she'd let *me* go to a women's college," Chris remarked after Mrs. Hamilton had walked out of the kitchen.

Elaine and Francis laughed a little.

"She'll come around, Elaine," said Francis. "Don't worry."

"She won't," Elaine said. She looked at a stick of unsalted butter lying in a serving plate on the counter. "But that's all right."

"And now on to bigger problems," said Chris, jumping up. "We haven't talked about what we're going to wear—"

"You'll wear these," said Mr. Hamilton, entering the kitchen with a large box. He opened it and took out three chef's jackets. They were starched and brand-new, with the insignia HIGH SCHOOL CHEF embroidered in red across the breast pocket.

Elaine stared at the jacket, touched the buttons, ran her finger over the embroidery.

"Do these puffy hats come in any other colors?" Chris asked.

"Excuse us for a moment, boys," Mr. Hamilton said, looking at Elaine. "I'd like to have a word with your sister."

"About what?" Chris demanded. "How come you're not going to dispense any fatherly advice to us?"

"Out!"

When the boys had left the room, Mr. Hamilton sat down at the kitchen table. He motioned for Elaine to sit down next to him.

"Listen," he said. "I want you to go upstairs and talk to your mother."

"I don't have anything to say," Elaine said stiffly. "She's made her position quite clear."

"Has she?" asked Mr. Hamilton. "Maybe if you go into her office and talk to her one more time she'll listen."

"She won't listen," said Elaine.

"Well, maybe you could listen," Mr. Hamilton suggested.

"I have listened."

"Have you?" Mr. Hamilton asked. He smiled pleasantly.

Elaine shrugged. She left the kitchen table and went upstairs to the office, where her mother was sitting at her desk, writing. She looked up when she heard Elaine.

"Oh, hi, Elaine. Just finishing up some copy here for tomorrow's paper."

Elaine stood awkwardly in the doorway, fiddling with her glasses.

"Why don't you sit down?" Mrs. Hamilton asked. She nodded to an armchair across from the desk. Elaine sat in the chair and looked at the framed photographs on the wall behind the desk, showing her mother posing with the House speaker, a chief justice, even the president of the United States. Her mother's law diploma hung in a frame beside a photograph of a bill signing at the White House. Mrs. Hamilton put down her pen.

"Dad said I should come up and talk to you," Elaine said.

"Did he?"

"Yes," Elaine said. She looked above her mother's head at the framed diploma.

Mrs. Hamilton turned around and studied the diploma with Elaine.

"Do you find it interesting?" her mother asked. She tilted her chair and looked thoughtfully at the frame. "That was a long time ago. But I remember the day very well. I was valedictorian and editor in chief of the law review. These were honors rarely bestowed on women, regardless of how much they worked or how much they deserved it."

Elaine nodded.

"You could graduate at the top of your class at Dartmouth, Elaine. You're very talented."

"I don't want to go to Dartmouth," Elaine said.

Mrs. Hamilton opened her mouth to say something but then closed it again. She looked at the papers on her desk.

"Maybe you'll change your mind," she said quietly.

Elaine looked at her feet.

"I never said you had to go into politics," said Mrs. Hamilton. "I only hope that you will find a profession where women have not been traditionally relegated—"

"But most chefs are men," Elaine whispered, clenching her apron in her fists.

"—or in the least you will not waste the opportunities made available to you. If you go to a two-year cooking school—"

"Smith College is a four-year institution," Elaine said.

"Yes. It's also a women's college, and I'd like you to study in a place with real-world conditions."

Elaine said nothing.

Mrs. Hamilton said gently, "You do nothing to dismantle male privilege by staying in the kitchen with stews and saucepans, Elaine."

"But I like stews and saucepans," Elaine responded. "It's my life's ambition to be around them."

Mrs. Hamilton shook her head and stared at the papers on her desk. "All my life," she said softly, in near disbelief, "I had to clean up after my brothers. I had to clean up after my father. All through childhood and adolescence, I had to do the grocery shopping and the cooking and the dishwashing.

"I hated to be in that kitchen," she continued. "When I graduated, my father would have forced me to go to finishing school if it weren't for that scholarship." Mrs. Hamilton shook her head at the memory. "And when I married, I vowed no daughter of mine would ever have to suffer the indignities of cleaning or cooking simply because she's female—"

"But I like cooking," Elaine said. "I even like cleaning. Don't you see—"

"Yes, I see," said Mrs. Hamilton. "But that doesn't mean I *like* what I see. And it doesn't mean that I can't want more for you, Elaine. You are my first and only daughter. Why should you endure the hardships that I suffered? You don't know for sure what you'll want to do in ten years. You might change your mind. And then it will be too late."

"I won't change my mind," Elaine said, but her mother was speaking over her now, delivering a speech about the ways in which culture reduced females to their biology, and about opportunities open to women outside traditional gender roles.

"All right," said Elaine. She replaced her glasses. "All right," she repeated quietly. She stood up and went to the door.

"Elaine," said Mrs. Hamilton, looking earnestly at her daughter. "You're still young. All I'm asking is that you think about the things I'm telling you."

Elaine nodded. She put her hand on the doorknob. She hesitated.

"Mom?"

"Yes?" Mrs. Hamilton was writing again.

"Whatever happens with college," she said. "I'm still going to that competition."

"I'm aware of that, Elaine."

"And I'd . . ." Elaine cleared her throat. She took a deep breath. "I'd really like you to come."

Mrs. Hamilton looked up from her desk, and an odd expression passed across her face. She swallowed.

"I know," she said. "And I really appreciate that."

20

The competition was held in the convention center at the university in New Paltz, where Elaine's mother delivered her victory speeches on election night. Those times, the hall was filled with balloons and confetti and neckties. There had been a live band and the popping of champagne corks. Now the hall looked different.

"Wow," said Chris when he saw all the men in toques and chef's whites milling around the blue carpet. In the middle of the giant room was a center stage with marble floors and spotlights that shone down on stainless-steel appliances. Ten kitchen units, each complete with sink, work area, and stove, formed a rectangle around a huge pantry station at the center.

"I didn't know there would be so many contestants," Francis said, watching the culinary students carry their knife sets into the hall while their instructors followed closely behind, giving last-minute preparation advice. Men and women in uniforms with CSNY stitched into the cotton carried in crates of fresh produce while important-looking officials in suits walked around with clipboards. Television cameras and rows of hydraulic seating surrounded the stage. Projection screens hung down from ceiling beams in every corner.

"I didn't know it would be so *big*," Elaine murmured.

"Good thing you're used to working in front of a camera, huh, Elaine?" said Chris. He looked around appreciatively.

Elaine walked away from her brothers to get a closer look at the kitchen stations. There was an ample-size table for preparation, a six-burner stove and microwave oven, three food processors, a meat grinder, and numerous pots and pans of every style and size. She ran her hand along the top of the cutting board and looked at the polished handles and shiny gooseneck faucet of the sink.

"Can I help you?" A woman in a suit, with wide green eyes and a startling hairdo, stood by.

"What? Oh, yes, I'm Elaine Hamilton. I'm—I'm here for the competition."

"Audience members are to present their tickets by the—"

"No, I mean—I—I'm a contestant."

The woman looked puzzled for a moment.

"My *sous chefs*—they're over there," said Elaine, pointing to her brothers several feet away.

"Excuse me?"

"Them," Elaine said, pointing to Chris, who was checking out the back of his wraparound dress in the reflection on an oven door, and to Francis, who stood by the hydraulic bleachers in his baseball cap and sneakers.

The woman raised her eyebrows at Elaine.

"Who is your instructor?" she asked.

"I—I don't have an instructor."

The woman clicked her pen several times and stared at Elaine. She consulted her clipboard.

"What did you say your name was?" she asked again.

"Elaine Hamilton."

The woman flipped up a page on her clipboard. She looked startled.

"Didn't anyone tell you to change into your whites?" she asked. She pointed to an area cordoned off with a velvet rope behind the rows of seats. "You can change in there," she said. "And tell your—your brothers," she continued, squinting at Chris in the distance, "they must change as well. We'll be starting soon."

"Thank you," Elaine said. She went and got Francis, who walked back with her to the kitchen stations, where Chris was testing the faucets.

"Quit that," said Francis. "We have to change."

"Elaine, this is, like, the real thing," Chris said, biting his lip and looking around. "Everyone's going to be watching us. Everyone! We're on network television!"

A cameraman carrying a furry microphone on a long pole nodded and winked at Chris. "Don't get too excited," he said. "They edit out most of it." He lowered his voice. "But if you want to see where the big boys are, look over there." He pointed to a pair of gray-haired men in dark suits, sitting in the front row by themselves. They were frowning.

"Network executives," the cameraman said.

"What are they doing?" Francis asked.

The cameraman shrugged. "Scouting for talent, I guess. Are you boys competing?"

"She is," said Chris, pulling Elaine up next to him. "We're just the assistants."

The cameraman looked at Elaine and squinted a little.

"Well, good luck, kiddo. They'll be watching you."

"Did you hear that?" Chris said. "We could get our own show!"

"I don't want my own show," Elaine said. "Come on, we have to change."

They walked past spectators filing into the hall toward their seats, past ushers helping spectators, and past a crowd of chefs and directors and more technicians wearing headsets. They changed on the other side of a tall partition behind the rows of seats.

When Elaine emerged in her chef's clothes, she was met by another official with a clipboard, who assigned her to kitchen Station Four, a center station between Station Two and Station Six.

"Starting bell sounds in twenty minutes," a woman said, handing Elaine and her brothers name tags to pin to their jackets. Elaine returned to the center of the hall and was surprised to find so many seats already filled. There was a lot of noise and commotion as people of all sizes entered the convention center. Camera crews put the finishing touches on lights and sound checks. More crowds flowed in. People jumped up and down in their seats and waved.

"Where's Dad?" asked Chris, looking pale in his chef's jacket.

"He's right there, in the second row," said Francis. "It looks like he's yelling at Robyn."

Elaine looked out into the audience and saw her father. Robyn, Lynn, and Leslie screamed and waved. She waved back. The aisle seat was empty.

"Dad got her a ticket anyway," Francis told Elaine. "In case she changes her mind."

"She won't change her mind," Elaine said.

A man wearing houndstooth pants and carrying a clipboard approached Elaine. He looked at her name tag.

"Come this way," he said, leading Elaine and her brothers to a designated seating area by one of the stations. Chris and Francis stared at their competition, an assembly of other teenagers in toques and white chef's jackets nervously tucking in their dish towels.

"Elaine," Chris said, poking her in the back. "You're not going to believe this, but I think I see—"

"Shh," said Elaine.

"But—"

"Shh!" said Francis.

"Cameras will be rolling in about ten minutes," the man in the houndstooth pants was saying. "I am sure you have all read your competition package, but I'd like to state as a reminder that five judges will evaluate you on a fifty-five point scale in the following categories: serving method and presentation, portion size, nutritional balance, ingredient compatibility, and flavor. Kitchen and floor scores are a thirty-five point scale in which you'll be judged on organization and explanation—"

"Elaine, did you know this?" Chris whispered.

"*Shh*, of course."

"—cleanliness, task delegation, utilization of ingredients, timing, and techniques."

Francis took off his cap and ran his fingers through his hair.

"Don't worry," Elaine whispered.

"I still have to tell you—" Chris began.

"Shh!" said Francis and Elaine together.

"In five minutes you will approach your station," the man in the houndstooth pants continued. "Under no circumstances are you to look into your mystery basket until the sounding bell. At that point, of course, you may begin. You'll have four hours to prepare three plates and a dessert—"

"Are you crazy?" Chris cried out. "Three plates and a dessert!"

The others looked over and stared.

Elaine was feeling strangely calm. She looked over the heads of the contestants and toward the seats on the hydraulic bleachers and saw her father smiling at her. He waved and held up his thumb. Elaine smiled back.

"Please be aware that you are being recorded for television," the man was saying. "If the food network host asks you a question while you are working, we request that you respond in a direct and polite manner. There are talent scouts from the networks here today—"

An audible hum rose above the contestants.

"—but we will not be judging you on how well you perform for television. This, may I remind you, is first and foremost a culinary competition. I'd like to take a moment to emphasize skill, food knowledge, and respect for the craft—"

Elaine nodded.

"—over showmanship. Unlike other competitions, we recognize that all of you are apprentices, hopefuls who will someday go on to run your own restaurants—"

"Or schools," Francis mumbled to Elaine.

"—and are devoted to understanding the basics of French cuisine as the supreme example of the culinary arts. For this reason, young men and women, as we specified in the guidelines, we are not focusing so much on creativity as on a *proven understanding of the fundamental concepts in French cooking*. You need not spend your time impressing us with elaborate garnishes or fancy curlicues. We are interested in technique and flavors—the flavors of haute cuisine as demonstrated in the long-standing French tradition."

Elaine nodded.

Chris poked her again. "Elaine," he whispered.

"Not now, Chris."

"That's all, folks. In . . ." the man looked at his watch again. "In two minutes you can go to your station, look in your mystery basket, and begin planning your menu. Best of luck to you all." The man nodded, the contestants gathered near their stations, there was a countdown and cheers from the crowds, and the sounding bell went off. The competition had begun.

"Elaine," Chris panted, tying on a pink apron with lace trim, "you didn't say anything about a mystery basket."

"It was all in the competition package," Francis said. "The one you never read, remember?"

"I didn't want to worry you," Elaine said, opening her knife case. "You have enough to keep in mind as it is."

"Now that I have your attention," Chris said, "may I just point out that—"

But Elaine brushed by Chris and began pulling things out of the mystery basket and setting them on the countertop. One by one she laid down each item, separating the proteins from the vegetables. Here is a list of the items in the mystery basket, in case you are interested:

2 pounds of sea scallops
1 beef tenderloin
1½ pounds of *foie gras*
2 heads of Belgian endive
4 beets, 2 red, 2 yellow
1 pound of white mushrooms
1 jar of truffles
1 pound of tomatoes
5 Red Bartlett pears
6 large artichokes
16 ounces of almonds

Elaine took out a pen and picked up the clipboard on the edge of the counter. "We have to write a menu with these items," she said as chefs and their assistants began running around their stations like ants, chopping and dicing and slicing and setting up great pots of boiling water.

"Where's the butter?" Francis asked, staring into the basket. "Do they really expect us to make French food without butter?"

"Those are staples," Elaine said, pointing with her pen

to the refrigerator and the community pantry in the center of the work area. "Everyone can use that stuff. We have to make our own menu with the items we have." She looked at the illuminated digital clock on one of the projection screens in the corner.

"Chris, brush off the mushrooms and take out the paring knife. Francis, fill up that stockpot with water and set it to boil."

"Right away," Francis said.

Elaine looked at the foods from the basket for a moment. She stared at the main proteins and the salad greens, squinted at the truffles and the artichokes. Pages of Julia Child's cookbooks, thousands of recipes from *Mastering the Art of French Cooking, Volume One*; *Mastering the Art of French Cooking, Volume Two*; *From Julia Child's Kitchen*; *The Way to Cook*; *The French Chef Cookbook*, flipped across her mind at a rate that could only be described as the speed of light.

"How long do they give you to plan?" Chris asked, wiping a mushroom.

"Thirty minutes," Elaine mumbled. She finished writing her menu and motioned to one of the floor judges.

"Are you sure you're done?" he asked, flabbergasted. "You want to look it over one more time?"

But Elaine was already preparing the scallops. Chris sliced mushrooms, and Francis started in on the Belgian endive.

"What are we making?" he asked Elaine, rinsing leaves.

"You'll see."

The three of them set to work. The cameras moved around the student chefs, capturing different angles at different stations, and the audience cheered. Elaine instructed Chris to retrieve Madeira and shallots from the community pantry, and Francis plunged the red and golden beets into the boiling water. Francis sweated through his toque. Elaine worked swiftly but calmly. Chris julienned a beet into matchstick pieces.

Here is a copy of Elaine's menu.

First Plate: Coquilles St. Jacques à la Parisienne in Scallop Shells, Tomates à la Provençale

Salad Course: Salade d'Endives avec Betteraves, Vinaigrette, Parsley

Main Plate: Filet de Boeuf Braisé Prince Albert, Tomates Grillées au Four, Fonds d'Artichauts au Beurre

Pastry: Tarte aux Poires à la Bourdaloue

"You've got to work faster than that," Francis told Chris

as he reached for the other half of the first beet. "We've got three dishes to plate in four hours, not counting dessert."

"If I work any faster, I'll cut myself," Chris replied. He was humming to himself. A competition judge walked past and made a few scratches on his clipboard.

"Who does he think he is, snooping around like that?" Chris demanded, pointing his knife.

"He's a floor judge," said Elaine. She had just finished working some pastry dough into a ball and was wrapping it in waxed paper. She placed it in the refrigerator below the sink. "He's evaluating your coordination and technique."

"And your cleanliness," said Francis as Chris swept a few beet greens onto the station floor.

"Well, how do you like—"

Elaine told him to quiet down and dice the celery.

The three worked busily for the better part of the hour, simmering wine and vegetables in various pots, shocking tomatoes in cold water, paring artichokes, and juicing lemons.

Chris quickly learned to smile into the camera and scowl at the judges as they went by. The audience roared with approval. Because neither Francis nor Chris had much of an idea of the menu (even if they had read it, they would have understood little), Elaine explained things to them as she went along, and the cameramen zoomed in closely while she instructed her brothers.

"You want to be careful with those scallops, Chris," she said. "Simmering them for more than five minutes will result in a rubbery texture." To Francis, who was assigned to the artichokes, she said, "Preparation of this vegetable is exacting; the lower leaves must be broken off from the artichoke bottom in such a way as to lose as little of the meat as possible. After you trim the heart, you have to give it a preliminary cooking in *vin blanc* to preserve its whiteness, as it's prone to rapid discoloration."

Elaine was unaware that her style and method of competing and teaching at the same time had created something of a sensation. The cameras favored her over the nine other contestants, and they pointed their lenses and microphones at Station Four to capture her directions, which were well paced and organized. When the camera crew filmed other stations, it was generally to present the contrast—Stations Three and Six had already spilled and wasted a good deal of white wine; Station Two had let the tomatoes boil for too long. The chef at Station Eight was arguing with his assistant about crushing almonds, and someone at Station Seven was improperly trimming the tenderloin, wasting all the choicest parts. Elaine, oblivious to her competition—and the cameras and audience, for that matter—worked with her usual swiftness and precision. They were two hours into the competition, now, and Elaine had found a rhythm, had succeeded in ignoring the crowds and the cameras and the hustle as she did what she loved to do most in all the world—to slice vegetables for a *brunois*, to sauté shallots and onions in butter, to chop, to heat, to reduce. Elaine's whole life had led her to this day; in fact, she had been born for it. Under the warm lights and above the steaming saucepans, Elaine was *cooking*.

Chris said, "Elaine, I *have* to tell you something."

"Permit me the opportunity," Elaine said, removing the chilled pastry dough from the refrigerator, "to demonstrate the basics of the sugar-crust shell."

"Elaine, for pete's sake! Look over there!"

Elaine looked up from her *brunois* and her shallots and her pastry dough and saw something horrible. It was Croton Harmon. He was three food stations away, shaving beets with a mandoline. He wore a white jacket and dark pants like everyone else, but still, there was no mistaking his dark hair, the pale skin, and of course his one awful eye. When Croton saw Elaine looking over at him, he grinned. And winked his darker eye.

Elaine gasped.

"What the heck is he doing here?" Francis asked, putting down an artichoke and wiping his face with a dish towel. "Are you telling me that *he* can cook? Now I've seen it all."

"He's an assistant," Elaine said, her knife poised mid-slice, half frozen in disbelief, her eyes wide. Then, taking a long, shaky breath, she murmured, "To Marceau Etienne." Her shoulders slumped.

There was no mistaking it. Croton Harmon, the rotten fig himself, was taking directions from Marceau Etienne, son of the master chef and restaurateur, second in command to the finest culinary specialist in the Hudson Valley, and the very same son that Elaine had watched cook at both the fall and spring festivals. At this moment Marceau was chopping a mushroom so quickly that his fingers were a fiery blur of steel and vegetable. Diced mushroom pieces flew into the air and fell with astonishing precision.

"I have to use a food processor to produce a sixteenth-inch dice," Elaine murmured as Marceau Etienne finished a pound of mushrooms in less than ten seconds and twisted a handful into a corner of a towel to extract the juices.

"He's making Filet de Boeuf en Feuilletons, Duxelles," she continued, staring into the projection screen that had closed in on Marceau's knife work. "Observe his technique. The ease with the blade." Elaine looked down at her carving board. She sighed. A cameraman, noticing that activity in Elaine's workstation had ceased, rolled his camera toward her to get a close-up.

"It seems our number-one contender," a voiceover from somewhere announced, "has awakened to her competition."

"You jerk," Francis said, shoving Chris angrily so that he fell against a *bain-marie* filled with warm water. "Now look what you've done!"

"I was just trying to warn her!"

"What's next, Elaine?" Francis asked, breathing heavily. "The wine has nearly reduced to a cup. What should I do?"

But the world had collapsed on Elaine Hamilton. In the distance she heard the cries and the cheers of the audience, the booming voice of the announcer over the loudspeakers, the footsteps of the competition proctors running back and forth, the floor judges scratching at their clipboards. From far away she could smell her carrots and onions soaking up the butter. She could hear the distant bubbling of the reduction that was to become her *sauce à la Parisienne*. But looming more largely now, and eclipsing the lovely vision of her tart baking beneath a hill of kidney beans to hold the pastry in place, she saw in her mind's eye the horrible face of Croton Harmon the day he had crushed her videotape. She saw his face, then and now, white and doughy as a moon, staring at her with his terrible eye, daring her to go on.

"Come on, Elaine," Francis whispered fiercely into her ear. "Don't lose focus. Croton's just trying to derail you. And we can beat Marceau Etienne even if his father is a certified master chef and the most successful restaurateur in the Hudson Valley. Don't do this. We've worked too hard." He looked at his sister in earnest.

Elaine took a long, quavering breath. She thought of her mother, probably meeting with the committee for gender equality at that very moment.

"I'm scared," she said. Tears came into her eyes. She dropped her knife, and it fell to the tiles on the floor, making a clattering sound that echoed around the great convention hall, reverberated through the microphones the soundmen held over the cameras, reverberated and echoed everywhere, penetrating the depths of Elaine Hamilton's soul.

21

"So that's it?" Chris shrieked. "An hour to service window and Elaine's going to have her nervous breakdown right now? In front of a million viewers?"

"Maybe a thousand," a cameraman said, pointing his camera at Elaine, who was still staring straight ahead as if in a trance. "If you're lucky."

Chris snatched a clipboard from a passing judge and fanned his sister with it.

"Hey! Give that back," cried the judge.

"Do something," Francis shouted at Chris. "Help her!"

Chris kept fanning and shook Elaine's shoulders.

"Snap out of it," he cried. "Wake up, Elaine, wake up!"

"Say something," Francis said to himself quietly. "Please say something, Elaine."

Elaine blinked and said nothing. She stared straight ahead.

"I think she's having some kind of psychic break," Chris said, moving his hand back and forth in front of Elaine's face and peering into her eyes. "Elaine? Elaine, are you in there? It's me, your sister, Christopher."

Just then a figure appeared at Station Four. She wore moccasins and braids and a leather dress with a beaded belt.

"Pocahontas?" suggested a cameraman.

"Lucida!" Chris shrieked. "Lucida Sans!" He threw his arms around her.

"Evening, boys," Lucida Sans said grandly. "Imagine finding you here."

"Nice *ensemble*," said Chris, looking Lucida up and down. "The feather boa goes perfectly with that headdress."

"Thank you," said Lucida Sans, looking positively effervescent. "I've been watching from the fourth row up there. I wouldn't have missed this for the world."

She turned to Francis. "I didn't know you knew how to trim a *filet*," she said.

"Elaine showed me," he said, looking sheepish.

"You're hopeless," Lucida told Chris. "And if it's all the same to you," she continued, "I think I'd look a lot better in that apron."

"By all means," Chris said, taking off his toque and jacket and giving it to Lucida. Lucida buttoned the jacket and waved her feather boa at a judge with a white mustache and twinkly blue eyes sitting at a tasting table.

"Thanks, Mr. Nelson!" she called.

"Forty-five minutes left to service window," the voice on the loudspeaker announced.

"Would you boys excuse me a moment?" Lucida said. "I need to talk to Elaine."

Francis returned to his wine reduction. Chris went to sit with his brothers in the audience. The crowds applauded and whistled.

Four cameras from different angles pushed in closer to Elaine and Lucida. Lucida straightened the chef's jacket and removed her headdress and the wig with the braids.

"Long time no see," she told Elaine. She tucked a dish towel into her apron and looked around at the spectators buzzing in their seats and the judges walking around on the blue carpet. She observed the other contestants running back and forth slicing and mashing and calling out directions to one another.

Elaine stared at the ceiling.

Lucida washed her hands and dried them on her dish towel. She tilted her head in the direction of Croton Harmon, who was standing by Marceau Etienne as he sprinkled flour over his mushrooms.

"Tough break, huh?" Lucida said. "You have to admit, Croton's nothing if not versatile." She sighed. "And so handsome," she added.

Elaine said nothing.

Lucida picked up a chef's knife and poised it over a tomato. She leaned against the edge of the worktable and faced her friend.

"Look, Elaine," she said. "There are two things I have to tell you. The first is that I quit hanging around with Croton Harmon weeks ago. He doesn't deserve me, and besides, there's not enough room in New Paltz for both me *and* Croton Harmon's ego."

Elaine looked over at Lucida.

"The second thing," Lucida continued, "is that I missed you." She looked into the camera for a moment and screwed up her eyes. "Excuse me?" she said to the cameraman. "We're trying to have a private conversation here, if you don't mind."

The cameraman pulled back a little. Lucida turned back to Elaine.

"I really am sorry," Lucida said. "I didn't mean those things I said in the park. I was just so angry that you—that you just gave up. I hate it when people give up."

Elaine, about to give up on the competition, said nothing.

"But look at this! Look what you got yourself into, Elaine!" Lucida cried, suddenly waving her knife around. "We're at the New Paltz Convention Center! And you're competing against Marceau Etienne, the most famous teenage chef in the Hudson Valley! You're fearless, Elaine, you know that?"

Elaine's pupils returned to normal size and her eyes grew bright again.

"I am?" she asked, looking at Lucida.

"Definitely. You're the most fearless person I've ever known."

"Forty minutes to service window," the man on the loudspeaker called.

Lucida picked up a truffle and tossed it into a bowl of Madeira.

"Come on," she said. "Give me some instruction. We're going to fry Croton's eggs right here on network television. And beat the pants off that snobby Marceau Etienne, too, while we're at it. We're going to *win*."

Elaine frowned and picked up her knife. The spectators in the audience leaned forward, hushed, straining to hear what Elaine would say next.

"You've got to sauté the shallots and butter together for three minutes without browning," she said. The audience sighed and sat back in their seats. Elaine looked at the digital clock on the projection screen.

"Right."

"And Lucida?"

"Yeah?" Lucida turned around to look at Elaine, and the spotlight caught both girls' faces, which were projected suddenly on all four screens at once. Elaine's voice echoed throughout the convention hall.

"I missed you, too. At the risk of humiliation"—she paused, and took a breath—"you're the best friend I've ever had."

The girls embraced.

An explosive cheer rose out from the crowd as a thousand people clapped their hands and jumped up and down. The cameras nearly collided with one another to get the shot of the girls jumping up and down and hugging each other in their chef's whites while gripping their carbon-steel knives by their pearly handles. From somewhere at the back of the convention hall, Mrs. Elizabeth Hamilton slipped through a door, bent over to listen to directions from an usher, and made her way to the second row to join her family. She looked up and saw her daughter laying strips of blanched bacon across the length of a slit in a three-pound tenderloin and gripped the arm of a stranger making his way down the aisle.

"You see that girl up there on the big screen?" she said. "The one with the pork fat?"

"Sure I do," said the man. "That's Elaine Hamilton, this year's competition favorite."

"She's my eldest child," cried Mrs. Hamilton over the din, gazing at Elaine on the gigantic screen. "That's my *daughter*."

Elaine had lost twenty-five minutes during the competition, along with twenty-five points in organization and delegation after Chris withdrew from the competition to return to his family in the audience.

"Who is this stranger?" someone shouted from the audience, pointing to Elaine's new *sous chef*, carving tomatoes alongside Elaine and Francis at their workstation.

"That's no stranger!" someone else shouted back. "That's Lucida Sans! She named herself after a computer font! She's the most famous teenager at New Paltz High!"

"What's she famous for?"

"For trying to be famous!"

The crowd roared, loving every minute of it. Lucida rinsed the artichoke hearts and brushed the tomatoes with olive oil.

"Not too fancy," Elaine warned. "Skill over showmanship."

"Oh, what's a little showmanship among friends?" Lucida replied, tossing a whole tomato in the air and catching it with the edge of the plate. The audience cheered. Elaine basted the *filet* with the braising stock and began assembling endive leaves on a salad plate.

Meanwhile, Stations Three and Six had burned their scallops, and another team was disqualified for breaching the sanitary code. Eight teams remained for a while, and then a few more were disqualified for poor technique, lack of nutritional balance, and incorrect portion sizing. Eventually only four stations remained. The judges circled and observed, took notes and examined plates. Croton Harmon and Marceau Etienne, from Station One, rapidly plated a Salade d'Endives aux Noix while another team arranged Coquilles Saint Jacques Meunière on appetizer plates. Other dishes came forward—Endives à la Flamande, Filet de Boeuf Poêlé, Boeuf Bourguignon—and soon after came the desserts: Charlotte Malakoff aux Fraises, Gâteau in a Cage, Clafouti à la Bourdaloue. A contestant from Station Seven dropped a cage of caramelized sugar, and it shattered, and a towering *croquembouche* toppled into bits, spilling crème-filled puffs all over the marble floor. Two male contestants burst into tears. Soon there were only moments left to the service window, and three stations remained.

"Wow," said Lucida. "It's really happening."

Elaine spooned a light coating of red currant glaze across her Tarte au Poires à la Bourdaloue.

"When you carve the beef slices," she told Lucida. "They must be three-eighths of an inch thick."

"Why are we letting the beef sit for a few minutes?" Lucida asked, leaning over the braise.

A thousand people leaned forward and craned their necks in greatest anticipation to catch Elaine's words.

"To let the juices retreat back into the meat," Elaine replied. The crowds whistled and applauded.

"To let the juices retreat back into the meat!" they chorused. The cameras crisscrossed across the floor, the announcer boomed Elaine and Lucida's name over the loudspeaker, and the soundmen clutched their headsets.

"How does it feel to be nearing final service window?" an interviewer from Chef's Channel asked, pointing a microphone at Elaine.

"It feels fine!" Lucida said, grabbing his microphone and waving her feather boa at the camera. "Hi, Moms!" she cried.

Mrs. Fischburger Number One and Mrs. Fischburger Number Two waved their briefcases and held up a banner that read: NEW PALTZ SALUTES YOU, ELAINE HAMILTON AND LUCIDA SANS.

Food runners rushed the plates to the service window. Five judges sat at a long table. The first plate was brought out.

"From Station Ten," boomed the loudspeaker. "A first plate, Timbales de Coquilles St. Jacques. Traditionally made with unmolded chicken liver and *béurnaise* sauce, this dish has been adapted with scallops to make a dish of uncompromising taste and quality."

One by one the judges tasted the meal and proffered up comments to the chef.

"Delicious," said one. "Velvety."

"Excellent mouth feel," said another, and jotted something on his clipboard.

"I like the textures," said a third. "And yet there is something quite—I can't put my finger on it—something flaccid in the aftertaste. A cacophony perhaps. I'd have to take off a point for lack of musicality."

Judge number one tasted Elaine's Scallops à la Parisienne.

"Often served as a first course with a simple *pain de mie*, the Coquilles St. Jacques à la Parisienne is a creamy dish of scallops and mushrooms, wine and butter. It is often served with a white Burgundy or a good white Graves. . . ."

"It's quite flavorful," the first judge said.

"I appreciate the earthy tones of the mushroom," said the second.

"It accents the wine perfectly," said another.

"I don't think she chose to use white wine, actually," remarked a fourth. "What type of wine did you use for the reduction?" he asked Elaine, who stood at the judging table.

"Dry vermouth," Elaine replied.

The judge nodded approvingly and looked at the others. "That accounts for the dryness," he said.

"Remarkable," said the third judge. "Note the bursting colors of the Tomatoes Provençal. A notable accent."

Lucida jabbed Elaine. "See?" she whispered.

"Flawless," pronounced the first judge.

"Impeccable," chimed the second.

"Seamless," echoed a third.

The audience clapped and cheered.

The food runners brought out Marceau Etienne's first plate, Coquilles St. Jacques à la Créole.

"Splendid," said the first, after tasting a small bite.

"Wonderful," said the second. "Beneath layers of cayenne and garlic, the emergence of bay, the essence of peppercorn."

The third judge took a taste. "Very creative usage of scallops in a first course," he said. The fourth judge agreed.

The crowd looked worried.

So it went. Salads were brought out, Elaine's endive and beet with parsley, Marceau's Flemish-style endives with butter, eggs, and lemons.

"Muscular," a judge remarked.

"Punchy," said another. "With heat."

"And a whiff of musk," said another agreeably.

And then the beef entrees, aromatic with spices and red wine, glistening in their sauces.

"Excellent use of the *foie gras,*" remarked the first judge.

"Winey," said the second.

"Briney," added a third.

Station Ten lost points for using expensive *filet* meat for a Beef Bourguignon. The competition continued. Tasters tasted. Judges commented and nodded at one another. Additional plates were sent to members of the audience, and one sample of each plate was photographed for the *Hudson Valley Culinary Journal*.

"Look at that," said Lucida as a team from Denver unmolded a magnificent charlotte with almond cream and fresh strawberries.

"Risky for a competition," said Elaine. "But delicious."

The charlotte sagged right at plating. More points were taken off. Soon only Marceau/Croton and Elaine/Lucida remained in the ring.

"Well, here we are," Lucida said.

Elaine tried not to look at Croton Harmon.

"The thing I like best about this dessert," said the first judge, "is the extraordinary levity."

"And brevity," added another.

"I have always appreciated a fine sugar crust," said the third judge.

"The richness of the almond custard is a perfect counterpoint to the acidity of the lemon."

"And the pear rounds out the sourness."

"Squares it as well," said the first judge.

"Flawless in its presentation," pronounced the judge. "A tapestry of complex flavors. This dessert is a true accomplishment."

At this point the last dessert, a Clafouti à la Bourdaloue, was wheeled in front of the judges. Baked to perfection, it sat in a round fireproof dish, a model of simplicity.

"The simple country *clafouti*," one judge said, dipping his spoon into the dish. He took a taste and closed his eyes.

"Mellifluous," he said.

"The harmonious balance of milk and sugar, eggs and flour."

"Elemental," said the third judge.

"Delicious," said the fourth. "It's perfect. I can't find a thing wrong with it."

"Neither can I," said another.

"Uh-oh," said Lucida.

From Station One, Croton Harmon looked past Marceau Etienne, who was standing by the judges as they tasted his Clafouti à la Bourdaloue, and smiled at Elaine and Lucida. Elaine looked away.

There seemed to be a bit of commotion at the judges' station. They huddled together and checked their score sheets. Elaine had lost points in organization because of Chris, but Marceau Etienne had not been perfect either. A judge found his first plate too peppery, and the second plate, the salad, had too few greens to constitute a proper portion.

There was no further debate. The score was fifty to fifty, a perfect tie. A peculiar silence hung over the audience as the judges whispered and pointed with their pens, shaking their heads and scratching the backs of their necks. Croton Harmon combed his hair and several hundred girls in the audience clutched one another and wept.

"He's all yours, girls!" Lucida shouted into the seats.

Elaine stared at her cutting board. If she had looked out into the audience, she might have seen that her mother was sitting beside her father and her brothers, holding her breath with the rest of the spectators in the convention center. But Elaine was not looking in that direction.

"Ladies and gentlemen," the man on the loudspeaker cried, his voice booming over the audience. "For the first time in the history of the CSNY's sponsorship, we have a tie for first place. In a manner unprecedented, the panel has decided that a tiebreaker will determine the winner of this year's Young Chef's American Culinary Competition. Our two finalists will prepare a single item, a rudimentary example of French cuisine that represents a nation's uncompromised taste for quality and simplicity. This signature item must be prepared in a time span no greater than three minutes."

A thousand people leaned forward to hear what undisputed classic of French cuisine would be presented to the judges in three minutes to determine the champion of the year's Young Chef's American Culinary Competition.

"The omelette," the announcer called out. "Our contestants must present an omelette to the service window." A murmur rose above the crowd.

"An omelette?" Lucida asked. "How ridiculous! What could they be thinking?"

Elaine loosened her dish towel from her apron strings. She removed her toque, and then, to the surprise and horror of the crowds in the seats at the convention center, and to the great shock and dismay of the camera crew, Elaine Hamilton walked away from her station and headed for the chef's changing quarters behind the partition. Just like that, she was gone.

22

Lucida ran after Elaine into the changing area. She watched incredulously as Elaine removed her jacket from a hanger. She lifted one foot to the bench to tie her shoe.

"Um, excuse me," said Lucida. "But what do you think you're doing?"

"I'm leaving," Elaine said.

"Have you lost your mind or something?"

"No."

"Are you sick?"

"No," Elaine replied. "But I can't complete this competition. I forfeit. Marceau Etienne can take the title."

"Do you mind my asking why?" Lucida asked.

Elaine sighed. "I don't know how to make an omelette," she admitted.

"Excuse me?"

"I can't do it, Lucida. I don't know how."

"Are you telling me you are not able to whip up some eggs in a bowl and pour them into a pan?"

"It's my weakness," said Elaine. "No matter how many times I've attempted, I haven't been able to master this one technique."

"Well, can't you at least *try*?" Lucida cried, twisting her apron in exasperation. "I mean, Croton Harmon was *my* weakness and I didn't give up, did I?" She pulled at her feather boa and looked around, panicked. "At least give it a shot," she said. "There's a jillion people out there, Elaine. And they're all rooting for you."

"It's no use," Elaine said. "Anyway it wouldn't matter even if I could make the omelette. My mother doesn't want me to become a chef. I give up." She shrugged. "I'll just go to Dartmouth." She buttoned up her coat.

Lucida was about to open her mouth to throw a fit of gigantic proportions when something unusual happened. Something quite unusual and out of the ordinary.

A woman walked in. She was six feet two inches—very tall. She had curly hair and wore a flowery blouse with a scarf. She was quite old, but there was no doubt as to who she was.

"Julia Child!" Lucida gasped. "Look, Elaine! It's Julia Child herself!"

Elaine stared. The color drained out of her face, and she backed up into the hanger rack behind her, knocking over a pile of coats and jackets.

"Oh, nonsense," said Julia Child, and her voice was warm and high and warbly, exactly as it sounded on television. "I had to come and see the hopeful for myself," she said. Elaine stared back in horror, her eyes wide, terrified at the sight of her idol in living flesh right in front of her.

"The whole convention center is waiting for you, Elaine," said Mrs. Child. She smiled. "Indeed, *I* am waiting for you."

Lucida grabbed Julia Child's hand and shook it vigorously. "My name is Lucida," she said. "Lucida Sans. And you're lucky to be famous."

Mrs. Child looked confused. "The computer font?" she asked.

Lucida glanced at Elaine. "If you'll excuse me," she said. "I think I'll leave the two of you alone for a moment." Lucida stepped away from the changing area, trailing her feather boa behind her.

"Lucida Sans," Julia Child murmured. "Such an odd name." She turned to Elaine. "Well then, Elaine. You've made some wonderful food tonight. May I?" She lowered herself slowly onto the bench and motioned for Elaine to sit beside her. "The judges permitted me to taste your dishes." She paused. "Being a celebrity has its advantages," she added thoughtfully.

Elaine turned various shades of pink and red and purple. She struggled to breathe.

"The Coquilles St. Jacques à la Parisienne was wonderful," she said. "Just the way it tasted the first time I had it in Paris. Earthy and winey. What did the judges call it? Genteel? Such nonsense, don't you think?"

"Did you—did you like the Salade d'Endives avec Betteraves?" Elaine squeaked.

"Yes, I tend to find most vinaigrette too acidic. But yours was wonderful. And I didn't mind at all that your brother . . . or is it your sister . . ."

Elaine shrugged.

"Well, she or he did a wonderful job with the julienne," Mrs. Child said. "Just marvelous."

Elaine nodded.

"And what a wonderful choice to make the Filet de Boeuf Braisé Prince Albert! What else would one do with a full tenderloin but utilize the truffles and the delicious *foie gras* and the Madeira for a magnificent braise. Simple, delicious—and elegant. Bravo, Elaine!"

"You didn't mind the substitution of blanched bacon?"

"Considering the limitations of a market basket competition, not at all," Mrs. Child said. "Not at all."

Elaine managed a smile. She sat down on the bench.

Mrs. Child looked at Elaine sideways as they sat together. There was a long and uncomfortable silence.

"Would you like to ask me any questions?" Julia Child asked.

"I'm sorry?"

"Your questions," said Julia Child. "There were so many over the years. I suspect you've answered most for yourself by now, but I will tell you that the way to make a hollandaise is to be sure to slowly add the vinegar during the emulsification process," Mrs. Child said. "And to answer the question about boiling milk for an *anglaise*, it *is* important because heat gives the dessert that custard quality after refrigeration.

"When you brown your chicken for fricassee dishes, such as Coq au Vin," Mrs. Child went on, "you needn't be fussy about it. A light brown will do." She paused. "The *suprême* is the *filet* of the chicken breast. Your *terrine* was grainy because you left it in hot water for too long. I've made that mistake several times myself."

Elaine stared at Julia Child. Julia Child stared back.

"Your mother is in the audience, you know," she said. "She spoke with me just this morning on the telephone from her office in New Paltz. Oh, did we have a wonderful conversation—all about politics and cooking and feminism and the ratification of the Equal Rights Amendment. I may have cleared up a few ideas she had about women in the culinary field. I do wish *I* could have been more involved politically. I suppose it is my weakness. But we can't do it all in one lifetime, now can we."

Julia Child looked at Elaine.

"I think your mother had some alarming misconceptions about me." She smiled and patted Elaine's knee. "But we cleared things up, I believe."

"You phoned my *mother*?"

Mrs. Child stood up. "Now, I see no more reason for this drama, Elaine. Stop caterwauling. You must go out there and complete the competition. Your fans await you."

"I can't make an omelette, Mrs. Child," Elaine said.

Julia Child sat down again. She sighed. "Ah, the simple omelette. So simple and delicious. And yet it seems to give everyone such *trouble*. But it's really not troubling, my dear. There's just nothing to it."

"I know, but—"

"Twenty seconds is all it takes."

Elaine shook her head. "I've tried so many times."

"I know," said Mrs. Child. "And now you must try one last time. One last important time. For your audience. For your family and for your best friend with the purple hair waiting for you at Station Four." She looked at the exit to the changing area, to the noise and the audience and the convention hall. "Perhaps even for New Paltz," she added, looking vaguely alarmed.

"And if I fail?"

"You could not possibly fail," Mrs. Child said. "From the very beginning you have been a success."

Elaine thought this over.

"But just in case," Mrs. Child said, grinning devilishly, "I will now whisper in your ear a little piece of advice that the great Chef Bugnard gave me when I was attending the Cordon Bleu in Paris. Oh, did he make wonderful omelettes—the very embodiment of deliciousness, I cannot tell you."

She took Elaine's hand. "I haven't told anyone this advice, I do not believe," she said. She grinned. And right then and there Julia Child whispered something valuable, something wise and helpful and fascinating, into Elaine's ear. Nobody else was fortunate enough to overhear this advice, so it cannot be written down. Only Elaine heard Julia Child's words. She is the only one who will ever know.

Elaine emerged from the changing area to an explosion of applause, cheers, and whistles.

"Our hero of epicurean delights, this year's hopeful winner of the Young Chef's American Culinary Competition," the man on the loudspeaker boomed, "has finally returned for the last leg of the competition." Cheers rang out loudly, and the camera moved in for a closeup of Elaine walking back to Station Four to greet Lucida and Francis.

"Well, it's about time," said Lucida. "You really had us frightened for a moment there."

Francis grinned and straightened his paper toque.

"And now, the crowning moment of the Hudson Valley's fourteenth Young Chef's American Culinary Competition, sponsored by the Culinary School of New York, the two remaining contenders for the title will prepare one of France's staple meals—the humble omelette."

Everyone applauded. Some people in the audience held up a banner that read NEW PALTZ LOVES YOU, ELAINE HAMILTON.

"At the start of the clock the contestants will have exactly three minutes to prepare and plate an omelette for the judges to evaluate. You will receive points for portion size, presentation, flavor and texture, and of course, measure of doneness."

Croton Harmon stood beside Marceau Etienne at Station One. Marceau Etienne looked straight ahead, his face expressionless. Croton Harmon stood between the cameras and looked over at Lucida and Elaine.

"You'll never do it, Elaine Hamilton," Croton Harmon cried out suddenly. The audience booed and whistled. "Marceau Etienne has been working with his father at Jus Lié for five years. He makes omelettes every morning. You were smart to consider forfeiting the title. Give it up, Elaine. Give up!"

Lucida threw a slotted spoon in the direction of Station One. "He shaves his chest hairs!" she screamed at the cameras.

"Lucida, please," said Elaine. "Stop caterwauling."

"On your mark," boomed the loudspeaker. "Ten seconds to the start!"

"Give up!" called Croton.

The audience jeered and booed Croton Harmon, which didn't seem to bother him.

"Nine!"

"Are you ready?" Francis whispered to Elaine.

"I'll run to the pantry for the eggs," said Lucida.

"Seven!"

"How many do we need?" Francis asked Elaine gently.

"Five!"

The crowds started to chant Elaine's name. The sound was deafening.

"Four!"

"Elaine, how many eggs?" Lucida shrieked.

"Three seconds!"

Elaine straightened her shoulders and pushed her glasses up closer on her face. "Three," she whispered. Her voice was hoarse.

The bell went off. Lucida ran to the community pantry and returned with the eggs. Francis set the burner on a high heat.

"What pan, Elaine?" Lucida asked.

"Twenty-four chef's iron," Elaine replied softly, "bottom diameter seven inches."

Elaine broke the eggs, one after the next, with one

hand, into the bowl. It was as though she were working in slow motion. Francis handed her the salt and pepper, and she whipped them together.

"That's right," Julia whispered, from her place in the audience, "not more than thirty to forty vigorous strokes."

At the thirty-ninth stroke, Elaine stopped. Lucida handed Elaine a tablespoon of butter on a saucer, and Elaine dropped it into the pan. As the butter melted, she tilted the pan in all directions to film the sides. She waited for the foam to subside.

"It is only when the butter is at the appropriate temperature," said the man on the loudspeaker, "and is at the point of turning color, that the pan is truly hot enough to receive the eggs."

Elaine poured the egg mixture into the pan.

"Twenty seconds left to service window," called the man on the loudspeaker.

A camera moved in and focused on both omelettes—Marceau/Croton and Elaine/Lucida/Francis. Elaine allowed the eggs to settle in the pan for three seconds in order to form a film of coagulated egg at the bottom.

"You got it, Elaine," Francis whispered under his breath.

At this point Elaine worked swiftly, and a thin line of

sweat trickled down her brow. She grasped the handle of the pan with both hands and vigorously jerked it back and forth. Meanwhile, at Station One, Marceau Etienne was doing exactly the same thing.

In one sharp pull, Elaine threw the eggs against the far lip of the pan to get ready to flip it to the other side. This was the most difficult part, the part that thus far in Elaine's cooking career had always resulted in one disaster or another. She took a deep breath. Time suspended a moment. The digital numbers on the clock pulsed by slowly as the audience drew in their collective breaths and clutched their collective breasts in anticipation of what was certainly going to be the most important L'Omelette Roulée—rolled omelette—New Paltz, perhaps even the world, had ever seen.

Julia Child whispered something to a technician, who whispered something into his walkie-talkie, which was heard through the headset of a cameraman, who swiveled his camera around to focus on the face of Elizabeth Hamilton sitting with her family. At precisely the same moment Elaine was increasing the angle of the pan just slightly, she looked up and saw her mother's face, enormous and gigantic, reflected on four tremendous projection screens in every corner of the convention center. Wherever

Elaine looked, no matter the direction, it seemed, her mother was looking at her, smiling, nodding and smiling, and showering her with pride and admiration. Elizabeth Jane Hamilton was looking at her eldest child and only daughter with an expression that could only be described as the face of love.

"I believe in you," she seemed to be saying. "I believe in you, and I love you."

A cry echoed out over the New Paltz Convention Center as Elaine jerked the pan, loosening the omelette so that it leaped upward and flew ten feet in the air, turning over and over itself like an Olympic diver sprung from the high board. Suspended in near slow-motion, it hovered above the pan and Lucida and Francis, above the crowds and the camera and Elaine herself before catching the edge of an air current and swaying over itself, then falling and turning once, then twice, then three times before drifting down to earth, toward the edge of the pan, where it fell with a gentle nod as Elaine, holding the plate in her left hand and the handle in her right, transferred the omelette to the center of the serving dish. She let out her breath.

The noise of the crowd was immeasurable. The crowds screamed and chanted Elaine's name and waved their banners madly. Marceau Etienne and Croton Harmon, distracted by the pandemonium in the audience, turned away from their omelette for a moment too long and it first began to smoke, then burn.

Lucida dusted the top of the omelette with a little parsley. Francis handed the platter to the judges.

"A paragon of virtue," the man on the loudspeaker pronounced, after all five judges had examined the creamy interior, sampled the subtle flavors that could only be described as exquisite, and devoured an omelette that was, without a doubt, for the first time in Elaine Hamilton's life, utterly, impossibly perfect.

The crowd rushed the stage, jumping up and down and hugging one another and screaming Elaine's and Lucida's names. Francis hugged Lucida, and then he kissed her, right in front of the cameras. The crowd applauded.

"We have a victory," the man on the loudspeaker cried. The president of the Culinary School of New York, a certified master chef, walked down to the center of the workstation, and there, with the spotlight on him and Elaine, he took the microphone and handed her a large trophy.

"Ladies and gentlemen," he began. "In honor of the fourteenth Young Chef's American Culinary Competition, we would like to congratulate—"

"Tell me," Elaine said, leaning over to Lucida, who had her arm around Francis. "How did Julia Child—how did she *know*?"

"Whoever heard of writing a letter and not mailing it, anyway?" Lucida said, holding up a bobby pin and a paper clip in front of Elaine. She beamed at the camera. She waved at her mothers and held up Francis's hand, and pointed, and beamed again.

"—Elaine Hamilton, the national champion—"

"That's my girl," Julia Child said to herself, looking around with great pleasure at the crowds. "We knew you could do it. *Bon appétit!*"

Elaine ran off, trophy in hand, to meet her family. There is no need to describe the joy and the triumph of the celebrations that went on after this. You can imagine them for yourself.

Dear Julia,

Thank you very much for attending the fourteenth annual Young Chef's American Culinary Competition. It was an honor to meet you and receive your kind words of encouragement.

I am writing to let you know that I will be attending Smith College, in Massachusetts, in the fall. After this I plan on utilizing my scholarship prize to enroll in the Cordon Bleu in Paris to further my culinary training.

My mother and I speak every day now, and we are developing what my father would characterize as a "close but careful relationship." I am not entirely sure what he means by this except to say that my mother tried my *Pot au Feu* the other night and said, "Delicious, Elaine. Just delicious."

By the way, when it comes to the *Pot au Feu*, would you recommend *Sauce Alsacienne* over *Sauce Nenette* if there is a heavier emphasis on the flavors of the stewing hen, or do you think a *Coulis de Tomates* is an acceptable alternative? I seem to lack clarity in this arena, if you will forgive me.

Yours sincerely,

Elaine Hamilton

Epilogue

What happened after that? The Hamilton family went about their ways. At the time of this writing, Elaine is busily preparing Thon à la Provençale in the community dining area at Smith College in Northampton, Massachusetts. Elizabeth Hamilton is sitting at her office in New Paltz writing a letter to Elaine encouraging her to take a few courses on Gender Politics and the Law. Lynn is helping Robyn and Leslie sound out words in the low-calorie cookbook. And Chris is monitoring Mr. Hamilton's new diet plan.

Croton Harmon? He is planning his next scheme, no doubt. Rotten figs like him never get much better, unfortunately. They tend to grow up and become more rotten. But we will hold a candle for him anyway, in hopes that he finds himself and realizes the error of his ways.

Lucida Sans and Francis Hamilton are in love. Which is always very nice.

As are happy endings. *Bon appétit*!

Acknowledgments

I am deeply thankful to my friend Mary Ward Juno, who was an amazing source of inspiration at the crucial early stage of the writing process. I will be forever grateful to her, especially for the purple feather boa. I am also indebted to several members of the staff at Greenwillow Books for their thoughtful advice on early drafts of this manuscript: Sarah Cloots, Steve Geck, and Martha Mihalick. Lois Adams took me through the copyedit with incredible patience and kindness, Sylvie Le Floc'h created delectable jacket and page designs and found a handwriting font that "grows" (while keeping an eye on my French at the same time), and Virginia Duncan never even once intimated that writing one book per decade is not exactly sound business sense. Many thanks to Daphne Scholz of Bierkraft, in Park Slope, Brooklyn, for sharing her knowledge of artisanal cheeses, and to Jessica Applestone, of Fleisher's Meats in Rhinebeck, for her discussion of the tenderloin. Larry Marcelle helped me figure out all things crane, water tower, and farm animal, and Steven DeMaio, great friend and editor, brought his excellent writer's sensibility and meticulous editing talents to innumerable drafts and revisions. As always, I owe him an immeasurable debt of gratitude. Finally, I'd like to thank Lynn Mills Eckert, whose belief in this book never wavered, and who provided support and encouragement even during the darkest of car rides, at those unspeakably early hours, all the way to the Metro North station.